KINDLED

THE KINDRED SERIES, BOOK 3

ERICA STEVENS

ALSO FROM THE AUTHOR

Books written under the pen name

Erica Stevens

The Coven Series

Nightmares (Book 1)

The Maze (Book 2)

Dream Walker (Book 3)

The Captive Series

Captured (Book 1)

Renegade (Book 2)

Refugee (Book 3)

Salvation (Book 4)

Redemption (Book 5)

Broken (The Captive Series Prequel)

Vengeance (Book 6)

Unbound (Book 7)

The Kindred Series

Kindred (Book 1)

Ashes (Book 2)

Kindled (Book 3)

Inferno (Book 4)

Phoenix Rising (Book 5)

The Fire & Ice Series

Frost Burn (Book 1)

Arctic Fire (Book 2)

Scorched Ice (Book 3)

The Ravening Series

The Ravening (Book 1)

Taken Over (Book 2)

Reclamation (Book 3)

The Survivor Chronicles

The Upheaval (Book 1)

The Divide (Book 2)

The Forsaken (Book 3)

The Risen (Book 4)

Books written under the pen name
Brenda K. Davies

The Vampire Awakenings Series

Awakened (Book 1)

Destined (Book 2)

Untamed (Book 3)

Enraptured (Book 4)

Undone (Book 5)

Fractured (Book 6)

Ravaged (Book 7)

Consumed (Book 8)

Unforeseen (Book 9)

Forsaken (Book 10)

Relentless (Book 11)

Coming Fall 2020

The Alliance Series

Eternally Bound (Book 1)

Bound by Vengeance (Book 2)

Bound by Darkness (Book 3)

Bound by Passion (Book 4)

Bound by Torment (Book 5)

Coming Spring 2020

The Road to Hell Series

Good Intentions (Book 1)

Carved (Book 2)

The Road (Book 3)

Into Hell (Book 4)

Hell on Earth Series

Hell on Earth (Book 1)

Into the Abyss (Book 2)

Kiss of Death (Book 3)

The Edge of the Darkness

Coming Summer 2020

Historical Romance

A Stolen Heart

CHAPTER ONE

"You going to stand out here all night?"

Devon slid out from behind the tree. Chris turned to him and shook his head slightly. Chris hadn't known exactly where Devon was, but he'd known he was nearby. "If that's what it takes."

Chris rolled his eyes as he shoved his hands in his pockets and came across his front yard toward Devon. "Cassie will be pissed if she knows you're watching over her."

"She already knows." Chris's dark blond eyebrows shot up questioningly. "She may not want it to be true, but we are still connected. Though it was only a few drops, her blood is still inside me. There has *always* been a bond between us, there always will be. How is she?"

Chris's face darkened as he glanced at Cassie's house. They had buried her grandmother today, the only family Cassie had left in this world, and the only woman who had given Chris an ounce of love and caring. "The same," he muttered. "Unfortunately."

Devon knew exactly how Chris felt. Since her grandmother's murder Cassie had been withdrawn, furious, and lost. She'd turned against the ones she loved, especially him; she wanted nothing more to do with him, or his love for her. It broke his non-beating heart, but he couldn't find it in himself to blame her for it. He hated himself for what had been done to her and her family. He may not have killed her grandmother, but this was his fault.

He had helped turn Julian into the vicious killer he was. When Devon had turned against his kind, spurning human blood, Julian had been infuriated with his decision and determined to turn Devon back, or exact his revenge. "Are you going to stand out here in the snow all night, or do vampires not feel the cold?" Chris inquired.

"We feel it," Devon replied with a wry smile. "The same as you."

"Good to know, why don't you come in? You can be scary stalker guy from my porch."

"Scary stalker guy?"

Chris grinned at him, but his smile didn't reach his haunted, sapphire eyes. "Yeah, you're definitely getting there."

Devon scowled at him, but he followed Chris as he trudged through the snow to his porch. The beat up screen door squeaked as Chris opened it. "Come on in," Chris invited.

Devon stomped his shoes off before entering the porch area, though once he got inside he didn't know why he had bothered to clean them off. The worn floorboards and sagging wood were covered with a layer of dirt. It was obvious Chris's mother didn't have the money for upkeep, or feel like being bothered to clean. Devon's gaze fell on the bags of cans and bottles piled in the corner, cases of empty beer bottles sat next to them. She would have a lot more money if she bothered to return the cans and bottles, which he realized now was the source of the smell. No wonder Chris had spent so much time at Cassie's house, Devon wouldn't like to spend much time here either, and he had only made it as far as the porch.

He turned back to the storm glass in the screen door, his gaze focused on Cassie's house. He refused to let it be out of his sight. "You can see her house from here." Chris strode over and pulled the cord on a set of curtains, revealing a few small windows in the enclosure. Chris grinned at him, grabbed an old chair and shoved it in front of the window. "Make yourself comfortable, I'm going to put on a pot of coffee. I don't suppose I could interest you in any?"

Though he didn't need the liquid for nourishment, he wouldn't mind the warmth. "Coffee sounds good."

Chris's eyes widened as his mouth parted. "You can drink it?" he blurted out.

Devon couldn't help but grin at him. "I may not have to have it to survive, but it's not going to hurt me."

Chris grinned sheepishly before nodding and ducking through the doorway. Devon leaned forward in his seat and folded his hands before him as he stared at Cassie's house through the dirty windows. The light in her room was off, but she was still awake. He could feel her presence, the anger and suffering filling her. He ached to hold her, or to somehow take it all back. But he couldn't do either of those things, so he had to settle for making sure she didn't do something crazy, like get herself killed. That wasn't going to be easy.

Cassie suddenly appeared at her window, her hands fumbled hastily with the latch as she shoved and pushed at the glass. Devon rose swiftly, prepared to go and stop her. He would drag her kicking and screaming back into the house if that was what it took. She hated him already; he didn't care if she hated him even more as long as it kept her safe. If it came down to it he would handcuff her to her bed in order to keep her safe.

Cassie finally flung the window open, leaning out she inhaled deep breaths of the chilly night air. Her hands clung to the sill; her hair fell in golden waves before her. She was shivering fiercely, but he was certain it wasn't from the cold. Shuddering again, she hung low over the window as she slipped to her knees.

Devon's hands fisted as he fought the urge to go to her, to hold her and console her.

"She's not crying."

Devon turned, surprised to find Chris standing beside him. He'd been so focused on Cassie he hadn't noticed Chris's return. "How can you be sure?" Devon demanded gruffly.

Chris turned to him, his gaze bearing the haunted look that seemed to shimmer permanently in his eyes now. Devon was beginning to hate that look, mainly because it seemed as if Chris was losing hope for Cassie. And if Chris lost hope, he didn't know what he was going to do. For their entire lives Chris had been Cassie's shoulder to lean on. No, Chris couldn't lose hope for her, because if he did, then Devon might have to admit all hope was lost.

"She doesn't cry, or at least she hasn't yet. She's too infuriated for that." Chris handed him a cup of steaming coffee. "I figured you would be a black kind of guy."

"I am. If she's not crying, then what is she doing?"

"Trying to breathe." At Devon's questioning glance, Chris waved briefly at the window. "It's too much hatred; she doesn't know how to handle it. She can't breathe through it."

"I see."

"I don't." Chris pulled up another chair. Sitting down, he blew on his coffee as he propped up his feet. "She thinks she can

Devon leaned back in his chair and folded his arms over his chest as he glanced at Chris again. He was surprised to realize Chris was perhaps the first true friend he'd ever had. It was a weird thing to realize. It was a weird thing to *have*. But Chris was on his side. Devon didn't fool himself into thinking Chris would choose *him* over Cassie, but Chris would fight for him, and he would not turn against him. It was a good thing to know, and something he was exceptionally grateful for.

"Thank you," he told him.

Chris flashed him a smile. "Don't go getting all sentimental on me you big bad vamp." Devon chuckled as he propped his feet up beside Chris's. Though he would have preferred to have been in Cassie's bed, curled up next to her, this was far better than standing outside in the cold. At least he wasn't alone here. "You know, before all this happened, I'd thought she would end up joining you."

Devon nearly toppled out of the chair. "What?"

Chris grinned at him as he shrugged absently. "I'm not a fool, I see what goes on between you two, and no matter how hard I try to keep the emotions blocked out, some things slip through. I know how difficult it is for you to be around her."

Devon stared unblinkingly at him, unsure how to respond, unable to believe what Chris was saying to him. "You don't think I would harm her?"

Chris's shake of his head caused his shaggy hair to become further messed. "Not at all. I think you love her more than you realize. You wouldn't harm her."

"And it wouldn't have bothered you if she decided to join me?"

Chris smiled wryly at him. "Before I met you I would have destroyed her myself, if such a thing had happened to her, even though it would have killed me to do so. But now I know you, and I know she won't be a monster. All I want is for her to be happy, and you make her happy."

"Not anymore," Devon mumbled.

Chris shrugged absently. "It will work out."

Devon wanted to believe him, but he wasn't too sure himself. "She didn't intend to join me."

Chris's frown intensified. "You talked about it?"

Devon tried not to recall the horrified look on Cassie's face when he had broached the subject with her. "Yes."

Chris made an hmm sound in the back of his throat. "She never mentioned it."

"She had made up her mind not to join me. She probably felt there was no reason to mention it."

Chris's eyes were distant as he thought over Devon's words. "She will come around."

Devon chuckled as he turned to him. "Are you always this optimistic?"

Chris grinned at him. "No, I just know how she feels about you..."

"Felt."

Chris's eyes narrowed upon him. "No, it *is* how she still feels; it's just buried beneath self hatred and grief right now. She needs time to work it all out. I know Cassie as well as I know myself. I *know* she's still in there somewhere and she *will* come back."

"And if she doesn't?"

"Are you always so pessimistic?" Devon couldn't help but smile at him as he shook his head. "I can't let myself think like that. I just can't. It would mean I've lost her too, and right now I can't deal with that. So yes, I have to believe Cassie will come back to us, you should too."

Devon ran his hand through his hair as he mulled over

Chris's words. He was right; Chris had to have hope Cassie would come back to him. However, Devon knew it was better if he didn't. He couldn't allow himself to have such hope, not when he knew Cassie's decision was probably for the best. In the end they couldn't be together, and there was a good possibility he would end up hurting her, no matter what Chris believed. No, Chris had to have his hope, but Devon couldn't share it.

"Why didn't she intend to join you?" Chris asked.

Devon shrugged absently. "Her parents, and now her grandmother, have all been killed by vampires. She was bred to hate what we are. You were all created to destroy my kind."

"Yes, but she doesn't have to be a murderer."

"I know that, and so does she, but it's still frightening to her. Plus, she would also have to give up the sun and the warmth of its rays."

Chris was thoughtful for a minute. "Eventually she could return to it though."

"Maybe, but she would have to spend hundreds of years in the dark with no guarantee she could ever go back into the day. Just because two of us have been able to do it doesn't mean others will be successful."

Chris nodded as he placed his coffee cup down. "That would be awful for her, but I'm sure she would adjust."

"There will be no need for her to."

Chris smirked at him as he shook his head. "Man you're depressing."

Devon grinned at him. "There's nothing more depressing then being dead, which I am."

Chris laughed as he nodded his agreement. The faint patter of footsteps turned both their heads toward the door. Chris's mother rested her hand on the doorframe as she steadied herself, the ice in her glass of scotch rattled as she moved. "Christopher, what are you doing here? I thought you would be staying with Cassie, and *your* people."

Chris's smile dissipated as his feet plopped onto the floor. "Luther and Melissa are with her. I thought it best if I returned home."

"Oh, *this* is your home now? You never act like it. It's more like a storage area where you keep your clothes."

"Mom..."

"I have company," she interrupted briskly.

"Of course you do," Chris mumbled.

"What did you just say?" Her voice took on a nearly hysterical edge.

"Nothing, Mom."

"Don't you talk to me like that! I gave you life; I took care of you even after I discovered what abominations you and your bastard of a father were!"

Chris's face colored, his eyes flitted briefly to Devon as his head bowed down. His look in Devon's direction caught his mother's attention as she finally realized Chris wasn't alone. She turned toward Devon and the furious, alcohol induced glaze slipped from her eyes. Disgust twisted through him as the heady scent of lust began to emanate from her.

"You didn't tell me you had a friend here," she hissed to Chris.

Chris's jaw locked as his nostrils flared. She might be one of the most repulsive women Devon had ever come across as she sauntered forward. "You didn't give me a chance," Chris muttered.

She chose to ignore him as her gaze remained pinned on Devon. "What's your friend's name?"

Chris glanced apologetically back at him. "This is Devon."

"Hello Devon," she purred, thrusting her hand out. He chose to ignore it.

"*Cassie's* boyfriend," Chris added pointedly.

She licked her lips as her eyes raked over Devon once more. "Whoever would have thought it from little Cassie." Devon's hands clamped on the arms of the chair. "I'm sure you've taught her a thing or two. I could teach you more."

Revulsion curdled through Devon's stomach. Chris launched to his feet with enough force to make his chair skid back a few feet. "That's enough!" he barked. "Don't you have a *stranger* to entertain?"

Her sapphire eyes cleared as her upper lip curled. Devon rose and rested his hand on Chris's shoulder as he stepped forward. Chris's muscles trembled beneath his hand, his shoulders were set, and his jaw locked as he glared at his mother. "I assure you, I'm a far worse abomination than your son," Devon informed her in a low voice.

His words finally pierced her alcoholic stupor. The ice in her glass clinked loudly as she took an abrupt step back. "What do you mean?" she whispered. Her heart thumped loudly as she glanced wildly at Chris. Chris gave her a brief nod, confirming the apprehension and doubts rolling through her.

"Why don't you go back inside now," Devon suggested. Though he didn't use his power of mind control, his tone was compelling enough to make her step further away. Nodding rapidly, she ungracefully spun around and hurried inside.

Chris ran a hand wearily through his hair. "Sorry bout that," he muttered.

Devon squeezed Chris's shoulder briefly before releasing him. He turned back toward Cassie's house. "Lily's death really hurt you too."

Chris couldn't meet his gaze as he stared out the window. "She was an amazing person."

Devon shoved his hands in his pockets. "Yes, she was."

"Not to mention you and Cassie are killing me. I can't keep her tuned out, and you wandering around like a kicked puppy is really starting to get on my nerves." Devon wasn't at all amused to be associated with a puppy. "The both of you are enough to drive a person crazy."

"And you can't deal with your own grief."

"No."

Devon watched as the snow drifted down. It was beginning to stick to the sidewalks and roads now. From inside, music started to play. Apparently Chris's mother had decided to bury her anxiety in a party. Digging into his pocket, Devon tugged his keys free. He slipped the key to his apartment off and handed it to Chris.

"Stay at my place tonight." Chris's his eyes flitted down to the key in Devon's hand. "It's quiet there, and maybe it's far enough away you can escape mine and Cassie's emotions for the night."

Chris shook his head. "I can't leave Cassie."

"I'll be here. She'll be fine. You should rest; you're starting to look like crap."

Issuing a harsh bark of laughter, Chris shook his head. "That's the pot calling the kettle black." He took the key from Devon's hand. "Don't you *ever* tell her I did this."

Devon grinned at him. "I won't."

"Are you going to stay outside all night?"

"My car's at the end of the road. I'll be fine."

Chris nodded and shoved the key into his pocket. "So, where do you live?"

CHAPTER TWO

As THE FIRST rays of the sun broke over the horizon, Devon parked his car next to Chris's beat up Mustang. Compared to Devon's sleek new Challenger, the old Mustang looked more decrepit. He huddled into his jacket as he made his way toward the apartment building.

Punching in his security code, he pulled the heavy glass door open. He welcomed the blast of heat that warmed his frozen extremities as he made his way down the hushed hall. Most people were still asleep, though the scent of brewing coffee was beginning to fill the air. Leaping up the steps, he jogged to the third floor and turned down the hallway.

Reaching his apartment, he pulled down the spare key he kept above the door and slipped it into the lock. He was exhausted; all he craved was a warm shower and a few minutes of sleep before he had to drag himself into the ridiculous institution of high school once more. Thrusting open the door, the first thing he noticed were the loud snores coming from Chris. He was sprawled face down on the couch, drooling into the pillow he had grabbed from the bedroom.

Devon shook his head as he noiselessly closed the door. Chris had made himself at home. There were fast food wrappers on the coffee table, a couple cans of soda, and the TV was on. Though the furniture was all sleek, modern and expensive, none of it was his. The apartment had come fully furnished, something that was reflected in the high rent prices.

Not like he cared, money wasn't an issue for him. That was one of the benefits of having lived centuries with little care for human life. He placed the spare key on the table beside the door. Shrugging off his jacket, he headed down the hall to the master bedroom. The room was large with a massive California King size bed jutting into the middle of it. The paintings on the walls were seascapes with boats and lighthouses, they also weren't his. Tossing his jacket on the bed, Devon pulled his shirt off as he made his way into the bathroom. It was large with a big jacuzzi tub, his and hers sinks, and a separate shower stall. Though it looked inviting, he had never used the tub.

Turning the shower on, he set the temperature for as hot as he could stand it before stepping inside. The stinging rays felt good on his sore back and taut shoulders. A night in the car had left him cramped and sore, but it had been worth it to make sure Cassie stayed safe. He stayed in the shower until the hot water ran out. When it finally turned cold he stepped out, toweled off and dressed quickly.

Chris was sitting on the edge of the sofa, his head in his hands as he stared at the floor, when Devon returned. "Rough night?"

His eyes were a little bloodshot as he looked up at Devon. "I've had worse. Nice place you have here."

"Not my stuff. You could have slept in the guest room."

The pencil in her hand cracked loudly in the still classroom. She felt the heads turning toward her but she ignored them. Gathering her things, she rose hastily, not caring that the bell hadn't rung yet. No one stopped her as she hurried from the classroom, but she did hear a chair skid back, and she knew Melissa was following behind her.

She shoved the door of the girl's bathroom open. It crashed against the wall with a resounding thud. Slamming her books on top of the counter by the sink, she spun toward Melissa as she entered. "I don't need a damn watch dog!" she exploded.

Melissa folded her arms over her chest as she leaned against the wall. Her onyx eyes were relentless as she studied Cassie; her black hair fell around her shoulders in silky waves to the middle of her back. "Maybe not, but you're going to have one."

Cassie fought the urge to rip the sink from the wall, something she could actually do giving the mood she was in. She settled for just gripping the sink tight as she took gulping breaths of air and tried to calm her racing heart and shaking body. How on earth was she ever going to survive this? She wasn't, that was how.

Turning the cold water on, Cassie slipped her glasses off and splashed her face in the hopes of reviving herself a little. She turned the water off and lifted her head to look in the mirror. Hands fisting, Cassie had to fight the urge to smash her fist into it to destroy the image she hated so much.

Blinking rapidly, she lifted her glasses from the sink, and slipped them back on. The dark lenses eased the burning in her eyes, but every part of her body ached lately. She didn't know what was wrong with her, well except for the obvious. Shuddering, she grabbed hold of her books as she strove to ignore the bone deep, aching chill that had become a constant part of her.

"No one would blame you if you went home," Melissa told

her. Cassie shook her head and pulled her hood closer around her face. It didn't make her invisible, but she hoped it helped to hide her at least a little. "Cassie..."

She sidestepped Melissa and pulled the door open. Blending into the masses, she made her way down the hall with Melissa close on her heels. She slipped into her next class, and was relieved when Melissa didn't attempt to start taking Calculus with her.

It was a lengthy, tortuous day. She felt like she was walking through quicksand as she roamed the halls. Cassie limply slid into her seat at lunch. Folding her arms over her chest, she kept her head down and avoided eye contact with anyone else.

"Would you like me to get you some lunch?" She shook her head in response to Chris's question. "You have to eat."

She shot him a dark look. He stared back at her. "I'm fine," she grumbled.

He shook his head and shoved his tray aside in frustration. Loud laughter drew Cassie's attention to the other side of the cafeteria. Marcy and her group of followers were gathered around one of the back tables, laughing and talking eagerly. Cassie watched them, confused and fascinated by their behavior. Then, they broke apart enough to reveal an opening in the table they'd swarmed.

Cassie's heart lurched and her hands fisted. Devon was in the center of the group, sitting casually in the chair with his long legs stretched before him. He was leaning back against the table, his arm rested on it as he flashed a beautiful, heart stopping grin at Kara. His black hair fell around his magnificent face and illuminated the dazzling emerald color of his eyes. Eyes she could see in vivid detail, even from her position of fifty feet away. No matter how much she didn't want to see him, she still couldn't help but admire how gorgeous he was.

was about to push her Guardian further when Chris responded. "Yes, I'm fine."

"When can we go back in the field?" Cassie demanded as she decided to drop the phone conversation in favor of the one she really required the answer to.

"I don't think you're ready for that Cass," Luther told her.

"I'm in the best condition of my life," she retorted.

"I don't think you're *mentally* ready for it," he amended.

Cassie spun on her heel and stormed into the center of the garage. "I am perfectly capable of fighting!"

"I don't think you are."

Cassie glared at him as she grabbed her black hoodie and slipped it on. Pulling the hood up, she folded her arms over her chest as she began to tap her foot impatiently. "I'll be fine out there. I would like to go out tomorrow night."

"Cassie..."

"I'm going out tomorrow night!" she snarled. "You can follow me or not, it's up to you, but I'm not sitting on my ass anymore! I'm going out and I am *going* to find them."

She didn't plan to listen to any more of their arguments. Taking the side door she exited the garage, eager to be alone for a moment, but she knew someone would catch up with her soon. She momentarily contemplated leaving the sidewalk and main road, she was eager to get at Julian and Isla, but she couldn't bring herself to do that to Chris, Melissa, and Luther. They would be worried sick and they would follow her. Quite possibly to their deaths, and she couldn't handle having any more deaths staining her hands right now. No, if Isla and Julian came for her, it would have to be here, before anyone could catch up to her.

The chilly air helped to cool her heated skin and temper. Tilting her head back she stared up at the clear night sky. She wanted to be comforted by the twinkling stars, and beautiful moon, but she wasn't, and she probably never would be again. There was no joy in the beauty of the world anymore. Anger filled her as she turned away from the sky; she resented that something she'd once loved now meant nothing to her. Like so many other things.

Moving briskly down the sidewalk, she kept herself attuned to the world around her as she searched for any sign of Julian and Isla. She huddled deeper into her sweatshirt and folded her hands inside the sleeves. A car rolled up beside her, its headlights flashed over the few inches of snow on the ground. She turned the corner and kicked miserably at the sidewalk, she was spoiling for a fight.

Another car rolled up and its brakes squealed to a halt beside her. Cassie braced herself for Chris's wrath as she turned. Her eyes widened as Devon thrust his door open and jumped out of his car. "What do you think you're doing?" he demanded as he stormed around the car toward her.

Cassie took a step back from the exasperation radiating from him. Her heart briefly melted as it thumped with excitement. Tingles erupted over her body; her skin crawled with its desperate compulsion to be touched by him. Her body had been denied the sensation of him for far too long. Now it was frantic to feel the relief and pleasure only he could bring to her. Her mouth went dry as she took an instinctive step toward him.

He strode toward her forcefully, and with the fluid grace only his kind could possess. Power radiated from him, his emerald eyes were afire, and his hair was tussled and disordered. Her anger at him, and the world, suddenly sapped out of her. Love for him surged forth as tears burned the backs of her eyes. She rapidly blinked the tears back as he stopped before her, his mouth parted as his eyes quickly scanned her face. He for them to see how irritated she was by their presence, and Devon's. They had to think she was ok with this; they had to believe they could start to leave her alone. If they didn't leave her alone, she was never going to get her chance to go after Isla and Julian.

"Not much longer," she answered absently.

Chris studied her before turning away. Cassie took note of the few creatures stirring within the shadowy depths of the forest. If the animals were about then Julian and Isla were not. Unclenching her hands, she stroked her fingers over the stake she had in the waistband of her jeans. It did little to reassure her as she knew she would not be using it tonight.

Dani shivered and huddled deeper into her thick winter coat as the wind howled over the open expanse of the cemetery. Cassie stepped away from the tree as pity finally sank in past the shell surrounding her. "Let's go," she mumbled.

Dani breathed a sigh of relief as she scurried to her feet. Chris and Melissa looked just as relieved as they hurried to join her. Cassie turned on her heel, not truly acknowledging their presence as she made her way over the snow covered landscape. The snow crunched beneath her boots, but it was firm enough now that she didn't sink into it.

She was aggravated and frustrated Julian and Isla hadn't made an appearance. She had to draw them out and get free of her friends and guard dog somehow. Cassie glanced at the woods. Though she couldn't see Devon, she knew he was out there.

She rigidly turned away from the woods, unwilling to acknowledge him in any way. She knew ignoring him wouldn't make him go away, but she didn't know what else to do. There was nothing more she could say, or do, to make him understand the best thing for both of them was to be apart.

The best thing for her was to get this over with so she could be free of the misery and rage consuming her.

"Cassie?" She felt wooden as she turned toward Chris. "Are you ok?"

She nodded as she realized she'd stopped walking. "Fine," she muttered.

Shoving her hands in her pockets, she hurried toward Chris's car. She climbed inside and her hand twitched back to the stake at her side. She watched unseeingly out the window as Chris made his way out of the cemetery, through the center of town, and finally to her house.

She stared at the darkened house, allowing herself a moment to grieve for the warmth and happiness that used to blanket this home. Now it was cold and lonely, and only served as a constant reminder of all of the mistakes she'd made. She had failed miserably in all she had set out to do, and her grandmother had been the one to pay for those mistakes.

Cassie shuddered as she slipped from the car. Flinging the door open, she barely felt the heat on her chilled skin as she switched on the lights. "How about some food?" Melissa inquired.

"Not hungry."

Cassie tossed her coat into the hall closet and kicked off her boots. She felt drained, exhausted, completely beat, but she knew the nightmares wouldn't let her get any sleep tonight. She walked into the living room and plopped onto the couch. She turned the TV on, but she didn't watch it as she stared at the flashing screen.

Chris sat beside her and folded his hands before him as he leaned his elbows on his knees. "Are you sure you wouldn't like some food?"

She nodded as she absently flipped through the channels.

She wasn't looking for anything; she had nothing to look for anymore. She *was* nothing now.

Cassie curled her legs underneath her and rested her head on the throw pillow. She remained still, barely breathing as crashing waves of ire and absolute melancholy washed through her. She was a swinging pendulum of emotions and she hated it. She wanted off of the rollercoaster that was her life now.

She had to find Julian and Isla soon. She knew if she could just make them pay for what they had done to her grandmother everything would be better. Revenge *had* to make her feel better, mainly because she knew she wouldn't survive the battle, but it would be worth it just to make them pay.

DEVON WATCHED from the shadows as Cassie slipped through the halls with her head down. She had taken to wearing black hoodies in an attempt to keep herself hidden from the world. Though she may not draw as much attention from her fellow classmates as she used to, he couldn't fail to notice her. No matter how much she tried to make herself invisible, he would always be able to see her.

Her golden hair spilled out from under the hood she had pulled over her head. The habitual dark glasses she now wore blocked out the startling beauty of her violet blue eyes. Beneath the dark hood her skin was pale; the normal rosiness of her cheeks was gone.

She had always been lean with an athletic grace, but her weight loss had made the muscles in her arms stand out more, and the bones in her hands were clearly visible as she clutched her books to her chest. She had always been beautiful, shockingly so, and she still was, but it was a more refined beauty. She appeared older, more mature, as the youthful chubbiness of her cheeks had faded away to reveal the elegant planes of her delicate features.

Moving like a wraith, she didn't look at anyone as she slid into the girl's locker room. "What's with the sunglasses?" Devon inquired as Chris appeared at his side.

"She says the light bothers her eyes now."

Devon glanced at the fluorescents. They were harsh against his eyes, but he'd had a lot of practice with adjusting his sensitive vision to them. "You don't believe her?"

Chris shifted his feet and leaned against the locker next to him. "I believe she believes it, but I think it's just another way for her to try and hide herself away."

Devon suspected that hiding herself was part of the reason, but he knew it wasn't all of it. "She's still not eating."

"No, not much anyway."

If he could just get through to her, if *any* of them could just get through to her. "There has to be something we can do," he whispered.

"Doing the best we can. Nothing helps. And with Luther leaving...." Chris's voice trailed off.

Devon feigned surprise as he turned toward him. He knew Luther had left, but Chris, Melissa, and Dani still didn't know he and Luther had been researching about Cassie, and coming up against a solid wall of nothing. There was nothing about *any* of the Hunters like Cassie in the multitude of books Luther possessed. It was the most frustrating, boring experience of Devon's extensive life. Luther was determined to find something about them, even if it meant leaving at a very bad time in order to do so.

"Luther left?" he inquired innocently.

"Yeah." Chris ran a hand through his already disheveled hair.

"He got a lead on some Hunter in Texas or something. Said he had to go, but the timing is awful. Cassie needs all the help she can get right now."

Luther wasn't in Texas, but it was as good a cover story as any. Chris had no way of knowing Luther may come back with the *only* way to help Cassie. "That's too bad."

"What is this, a meeting of the minds?" They turned as Melissa strolled up to them.

"Yeah, you could say that," Chris replied.

She glanced at the gym doors. "You know if Cassie sees the two of you out here..."

"Three of us," Chris corrected. "And she's already in the locker room."

Melissa nodded as she shifted her backpack. "Good. I'm going to go in and make sure she's ok."

Devon grabbed hold of Melissa's arm, stopping her before she could disappear into the locker room. "How is she to live with?"

"She's just peachy," she mumbled, her gaze flitted to the doors as if afraid she would get caught doing something wrong. "She's the same there as she is here. Distant, unreadable, angry."

"Have you had any visions?"

Melissa's fine eyebrows furrowed as she shook her head. "No, not about anything important anyway but I'll let you know if I do."

Devon nodded as he released her arm. "Thank you."

With a low sigh she dropped her bag off her shoulder. "In all honesty I think she's nearing her breaking point."

"What do you mean?" he demanded. He glanced at Chris, who looked just as confused as Devon felt.

Melissa shrugged as she tossed her braid back. "I just don't think she can keep going like this for much longer. She's going to snap and either hunt down those two on her own and get herself killed, or she's going to have a breakdown. She can't keep shoving all of her sorrow aside; it's going to break free one way or another. We have to be prepared for that."

"What makes you think that?" Chris asked.

Melissa reclaimed her bag. "She's been living like this for the past two weeks. She can't keep going, one way or another everything eating at her is going to come out. I just hope she survives the aftermath, even if she doesn't plan to." She said the words in a flat monotone, but tears shimmered in her dark eyes.

"This can't go on anymore," he said firmly, though there was a tremor inside him. "I don't care if I have to lock her away somewhere, but this can't go on anymore."

"You can't do that!" Melissa cried. "She'd hate you forever!"

Devon's hands fisted at his sides. "She already hates me," he growled. "But I will make sure she lives, I *will* make sure she doesn't do anything to get herself killed! I will not allow her to continue to waste away. She can hate me for the rest of her life, but at least she'll have one."

Chris and Melissa exchanged troubled glances. "Devon..."

"No," he briskly interrupted Chris. "If something doesn't change soon, or if she tries to go after them, I will take her from here and there is nothing either of you can do to stop me."

Their eyes were turbulent, but they didn't argue with him; he wouldn't change his mind. She *had* to survive. He couldn't live through the loss of her life; he couldn't keep his sanity if such a thing happened.

"I think you're right," Chris muttered as he folded his large arms over his chest.

"Chris!" Melissa hissed.

He shook his head briskly. "No, he's right. She's on a downward spiral that will only end with death. We *can't* let that happen to her. She has to deal with her emotions and come to terms with all of this, and until she does, then *we* have to be the ones to keep her safe. Even if it means doing something she'll despise us for."

"Let's hope it doesn't come to that," Devon said.

"I don't think it will," Melissa said. "I don't think she's going to make it to that point. She can't keep going like this; it's only a matter of time..."

Melissa's voice trailed off as her eyes darted back toward the gym doors. "I suppose we should get our PE on. I'll see you in a little bit."

She hurried across the hall and disappeared inside the door of the girl's locker room. "Do you think Melissa's right?" Devon inquired.

Chris shrugged as he stuffed his hands in the pockets of his jeans. "I think she may be. Cassie is so incensed it's the only emotion I pick up from her. Come on, we had better get going."

Devon stifled a groan at the thought of having to go. He followed Chris into the boy's locker room though, and wrinkled his nose at the heavy scent of sweat and body odor filling the large, blue tiled room. He paid little attention to anyone else in the room as he changed quickly.

Following behind Chris, he made his way into the large gymnasium. His gaze instantly found Cassie leaning against the far wall. Her hair had been pulled into a loose ponytail that enhanced the angles of her thinner face. She'd changed into a pair of shorts and her loose fitting black tee hung limply on her slender frame. The sunglasses were still in place.

She looked like a lost child, out of place amongst the laughing, giggling girls gathered in a large group twenty feet away from her. His fingers itched to touch her, to comfort her. Melissa said something that caught her attention. Cassie looked up and nodded once before ducking her head again. A shrill whistle pierced the air. Devon turned as the two PE teachers entered the gym carrying bags laden with softball bats and balls.

His forehead furrowed as he stared at those bags. He hated being stuck in this school, hated being around these people. He was almost eight hundred years old and he was standing in a gym with a bunch of hormonal teenagers. His gaze shot back to Cassie and some of the annoyance melted away. For her, he could do anything.

They were shuffled around as they were divided into teams. Somehow he ended up on the same side as Marcy and Chris, while Cassie was relegated to the other side with Melissa and Mark Young. Mark had wisely stayed away from Cassie since their last encounter in the cafeteria, but Devon didn't trust him. Cassie didn't want his help, but Devon would take any excuse to beat Mark into a bloody pulp. He had been itching to do it ever since he'd first met the bastard.

"Cassandra Fairmont!" everyone turned as the girl's gym teacher barked Cassie's name. Cassie lifted her head, her forehead furrowed as she looked around. "You know the rules, no jewelry, no loose articles, take off those sunglasses."

He could feel her gaze zipping around the gym in a fleeting moment of panic. Then, she pulled the large glasses from her face. Cassie blinked rapidly before closing her eyes against the radiance blazing down on her. Devon took a step forward, he knew how painful such exposure could be and he wished to protect her from it.

Chris grabbed hold of his arm and shook his head as he held Devon back. "She'll be fine," he murmured. "She has to face the world sometime."

Devon tried to remind himself Chris didn't know, that he didn't understand and *couldn't* know the sting the lights could cause. Cassie's eyes were barely open to the harsh glare pounding off of the gym floor.

"Damn it!" he snarled as futility tore through him. "Damn it!"

Chris stared at him questioningly as Devon turned away. He grabbed one of the gloves from the bench and stormed into the outfield to take his position in left field. Marcy moved into center, Chris beside her, and Kara on the other side of him. Folding his arms over his chest, Devon waited impatiently for the game to commence.

They moved quickly through the first inning, and then the second. Devon thought his team was winning, but he couldn't be sure. The only sport he'd ever really been interested in was hunting, which he'd excelled at it.

Switching again, Devon was in the outfield once more as Melissa came up to the plate. The ball cracked off the bat with a resounding thud that echoed throughout. Devon ran for it but pulled up short as Marcy collided with him. Wrapping her arms around his waist, she laughed loudly as she hugged him. Chris retrieved the ball and threw it in time to stop Melissa at second.

Devon tried to extricate himself from Marcy's arms, but she was like a tick. Her leaf green eyes twinkled merrily as she grabbed his ass. Devon scowled at Marcy and grabbed hold of her petite shoulders as he forcefully pulled her away from him. She continued to grin up at him before turning on her heel and sashaying away. Chris's face turned ashen as he turned toward Cassie. She stood at the plate with the bat resting loosely on her shoulders as she focused on Devon.

There was a shaking inside of her, a whirl of confusion shivering through the bond that would *always* connect them. A shattering of spirit radiated from her. A shiver of foreboding crept through Devon; judging by Chris's reaction to her this was not going to be good. Devon wanted to go to her, to hold her, to get her out of there before she exploded.

She blinked, her attention once more returned to the game. She connected with the ball, a crushing blow that sent it soaring over their heads, before it crashed against the back wall with a resounding thud. It was a blow no *normal* human could have delivered to the ball, let alone a girl. No one moved to retrieve the ball as it bounced over the floor before rolling under the bleachers with a muted clinking that was exceptionally piercing in the still room.

The clatter of the bat hitting the ground drew everyone's attention back to her. She didn't run the bases, she didn't move. She simply stood there looking lost and heartbroken. "Freak!" Mark's word was low, but Devon heard it.

Cassie's shoulders were thrust back as she turned toward him. "Yes, yes I am," she agreed.

Walking away from the plate, she grabbed her sunglasses before striding out of the gym. The teacher didn't bother to stop her as she stood in stunned silence. Melissa turned toward them, her eyes wide and her mouth open. Then, she turned and fled the gym after Cassie. Devon had had enough of pretending to be a high school student, of pretending to be human.

He'd had enough of being alienated from the only person he'd ever truly cared about.

Marcy snorted and rolled her eyes. "What a drama queen."

"Shut up Marcy!" Chris retorted.

The boy's gym teacher opened his mouth to protest Devon's departure, but one sternly look from Devon caused him to snap it shut. He hurried into the locker room, not bothering to grab his clothes as he broke into a trot past the lockers. He blurred with speed as a sense of urgency drove him faster. He couldn't shake the tumultuous emotions radiating from Cassie, emotions he had never felt from anyone before.

Bursting free of the boys locker room, he quickly searched the abandoned hallway before turning and dashing into the girls locker room. He had a feeling he was already too late. He skidded around a corner, halting as he came across Melissa. Her dark head was bowed; she was holding Cassie's shirt.

She shook back her hair and lifted her eyes to his. "She's gone."

"Where?" he demanded. "*Where?*"

Melissa shook her head, hopelessness radiated from her as she held the shirt out. "I don't know I can't see it. I can't *see* it! What good are premonitions if they do nothing for me when I need them?"

"I'll find her." He ignored the scandalized looks of the girls filtering into the room as he bolted past them and slammed out the back door. An alarm rang loudly, but he didn't pay it any attention as he scanned the snow covered fields.

"Not here, she's not here anymore." Chris's breath hung heavily in the crisp air as he pulled up beside him.

"I know," Devon retorted. "I'll find her."

Devon didn't feel the cold against his skin as he took off across the field. There was only one thing he cared about right now, only one thing he could *feel*, and that was Cassie. Tuning out the rest of the world, he focused his attention on her. Scanning through all of the minds around him, he searched rapidly for the only one who mattered to him. The few drops of blood he'd savored from her when he'd closed the life threatening gashes in her neck, and the realization she wasn't far from him, allowed him to latch onto her mind quickly. He could feel her out there, running, fleeing, trying to escape. Trying to do the impossible and outrun herself.

Reaching the woods, Devon allowed his power and abilities to swell forth. With blurring speed, he tracked her through the forest. Though there were still a few hours of daylight left, he had to find her soon. It would get dark early, and with the cloud cover there was a chance Isla and Julian would wander out if they sensed her alone. She couldn't be by herself right now, not in her state of mind. He didn't know what she would do, and it scared him.

Bursting free of the woods, he barely took in the cemetery as he dodged easily through the headstones. He could sense her amongst the cold stones, and he knew exactly where she was. Veering sharply to the left, he bounded across the snow, not feeling any exertion from his run.

Coming over top of a hill, he spotted her amongst the rows of granite. She was kneeling before the grave, oblivious to the snow coated ground against her bare skin. A small moan of despair escaped him as her anguish encompassed him. He slowed, unwilling to rush up on her. Soundlessly walking up behind her, he hung back as he waited for her to need him or to tell him to go. He wasn't going to leave her out here in the cold, and he didn't think he could handle being pushed away again.

One of her hands was on her thigh, the other rested against the name on the grave as she leaned toward it. Her sunglasses rested beside the grave. A subtle stiffening of her shoulders told him she was aware of his presence, but she didn't tell him to leave. He glanced briefly at the stone as she lovingly rubbed her grandmother's name, Lillian Rose Callahan.

"Someone left flowers." Her voice broke on the word flowers.

He glanced at the roses and lily's resting against the stone. Some of them were browning and wilting, but most were fresh and colorful. He had left a bouquet just yesterday. "Yes," he murmured.

A shudder racked her slender frame. Though she had to be freezing, he knew her shiver had nothing to do with the cold. Her hand slid away from the stone and fell limply to her thigh. "I haven't been here."

He didn't know what to say, so he remained silent, frightened she would turn him away again if he did speak. Her violet blue eyes shimmered with unshed tears as she turned toward him. Her full lower lip began to tremble, making her appear far younger and achingly vulnerable. His hands twitched to hold her, to comfort her. It had been so long and he needed her so badly, but she had to come to him. She had to desire him again.

"It's my fault," she whispered. "It's *my* fault she's dead."

A shattering radiated from her. Her suffering was heart wrenching and overwhelming in its force. It staggered him. She bent her head, and for the first time since her grandmother had been killed, she began to cry. Her arms crossed over her chest, she rocked back and forth as she sought to comfort herself in some way. Devon thought he should stay away and give her the time she required to grieve. However, he couldn't stand to see her in so much distress and not do anything about it.

In two lengthy strides, he was at her side and kneeling in the snow beside her. He was nervous she would turn him away again when he wrapped his arms around her. She came to him, sobbing loudly, barely able to breathe as her small hands curled into his shirt. Rocking her, he held her as she cried, and kissed her head soothingly as he buried his nose in the enticing scent of her hair. Holding her again, he felt the bones of her spine beneath his hand.

Pulling her into his lap, he bent over her, trying to give her comfort and warmth as she trembled and shook against him. Her tears seeped into his shirt and soaked the front of it. Despite his pleasure at holding her again concern for her safety, and health, began to fill him.

"Shh love," he whispered as he cradled her against him. "It's not your fault. You couldn't have stopped this. It is *not* your fault."

He smoothed her hair back, kissing her tenderly as he held her head to his chest. He rubbed her arms and legs as he tried to get some heat back into her frozen flesh. Her sobs abated but tears still rolled down her face. He had to get her out of here and find someplace warm.

Lifting her smoothly, he groaned at the feel of her wispy weight in his arms. Even if she didn't accept him back into her life, he was going to make sure she started to eat more. She curled closer against his chest as her hand curled into his shirt. The shivers wracking her grew stronger, the skeletal branches of the trees clicked louder as the wind howled through them.

He moved swiftly through the snow and broke over the top of the hill as Chris and Melissa rolled to a stop in Chris's car. Melissa jumped from the passenger side, grabbed a blanket from the backseat and hurried toward them. Devon took the blanket from Melissa and covered Cassie with it.

He followed Melissa back to the car and eased Cassie into the backseat. Sliding in beside her, he gathered her back into his arms.

CHAPTER FIVE

"You have to eat."

Cassie lifted her head as Devon appeared in the doorway of her room with a tray of food in his hands. She felt hollow and exhausted, but she didn't feel the fury anymore. It was as if the tears had burned it all away and washed it clean. She still felt the burning thirst for revenge, but the inner rage that had blazed so hotly before didn't blaze anymore. She tried to find it, for it had been what was keeping her going, but she couldn't summon the strength for it anymore.

She watched as he moved into the room. His shoulders were set; his body tensed as if he was frightened he would scare her away. Her heart flipped over; tears burned her eyes once more. Tears she would have thought had run dry by now, but seemed endless. She had been so cruel to him, so cold and unforgiving when there had been no real reason to be. Yet, despite all her cruelty, he had still been loving and caring to her today.

She didn't deserve him. She didn't deserve many things, she

realized. Placing the tray on top of her bureau, he turned toward her. "How are you feeling?"

Cassie shrugged as she twisted the towel in her hand and pondered his question. She'd spent over a half an hour in the shower but she was still cold. She didn't know how she felt emotionally, not anymore. She had been infuriated for two weeks, now she was just empty. She didn't know how to describe that to him. She didn't know how to figure it out for herself.

"You went home?" she asked quietly.

He looked down at the fresh pair of jeans and deep green sweater he hadn't been wearing before gym. "No, Chris grabbed some clothes for me."

Chris had been to his place? *She* had never been to his place. She had known Chris and Devon still talked with each other, but it sounded as if they had become closer than she'd realized. She didn't know how to feel about that. Though, she knew they'd leaned on each other when she'd so brutally shut them both out.

She rocked forward as waves of self-hatred crashed over her. "Cassie..."

She held up a hand to hold him off as he approached. "I'm sorry," she whimpered. "I'm so sorry."

"There's nothing to be sorry for. Cassie, listen to me, you did nothing wrong."

She wiped the tears from her face as she tried to stifle her sobs again. She had been crying for hours, how could there possibly be any tears left in her? "I treated everyone so badly, especially you. How can you stand to look at me?"

He came toward her and dropped to his knees as he seized hold of her hands. "Look at me," he ordered gruffly. "Cassie, *look* at me." She lifted her head and her gaze clashed with his bright emerald one. She swallowed heavily as love swamped her. He had been everything to her, and she had turned her back on him. She had blamed him for something that wasn't his fault, but was *hers*. She had cut him deeply, and there was no way for her to take that back.

"What you went through, what you *are* going through is an awful, brutal thing. No one knows how they are going to react when they lose someone they love."

"I was cruel though, mean..." her voice trailed off as she turned her attention to the window.

Her forehead furrowed as she tried to recall the way she had felt for the past two weeks. It was as if she had been a different person, as if something had taken her over and made her someone alien and cold. Someone she couldn't stand to be around, but had to live with every second of the day. She couldn't tell him it had been someone else in her body. Of *course* it had been her, who else could it possibly have been?

"I was someone I didn't recognize. But it was me, and I was disgusting. I never thought I could be like that."

His hands tightened on hers, his emerald eyes searched her face. "Stop Cassie, stop doing this to yourself, stop hating your-self. No matter what, I love you." She didn't deserve his love, not at all. He never would have turned against her, never would have hurt her in this way. "No matter what happens I will always love you."

"No," she moaned as she tried to deny his words. "I don't deserve it, *don't* love me. The people who love me die. They die *for* me, and they die *because* of me."

His jaw locked. "You did *not* cause your grandmother's death, and there was nothing you could have done to stop it. You are the kindest, most giving and loving person I have ever met. I will love you for eternity because you deserve every ounce of that love, and there is nothing you can do to make me stop loving you. *Nothing.*"

His hand slid firmly around the back of her head, his fingers entwined in her hair. "If you turn me away again, I'll go. It will kill me, but I'll do anything for you. But you have to know I won't leave your life Cassie. I can't. Not when you won't take care of yourself, and not with Julian and Isla out there. I will be here for you until I'm certain you're safe."

Swallowing heavily, she couldn't stop herself from stroking his magnificent face. It had been so long since she had touched him, held him, felt him. Today in the cemetery she had been too distraught to feel the bliss his mere presence brought to her. But now, the peace he gave her began to steal through her body as it seeped into her pores, and warmed her soul. He turned into her touch, nuzzling her gently. He was a man trapped in the desert and she was his water.

"How could you forgive me?" she murmured.

"I could forgive you anything. You forgave me."

He took hold of her hand, keeping it pressed to his face as she stared at him in confusion. "Forgave you for what?"

He smiled at her. "For my past, for everything I've done, and everything I was."

"But there was nothing to forgive you for. You didn't do those things to *me* Devon; you are different now than you were then."

"There was plenty, you just never realized it because that is who you are Cassie."

Wonder filled her as she gazed at him. Maybe she didn't deserve his love now, but she would do everything in her power to deserve it from now on. "I love you too," she whispered.

Leaning forward, she meant only to place a chaste kiss upon his lips. But they had been apart too long, and as their mouths met she felt the instant flash of heat. A rush of love rose up between them, and buried her beneath the tumult of emotions tearing through her. Devon's fingers firmly clasped hold of the back of her head.

She knew instantly she'd made a mistake. Now she was accepting him again; his desire was more intense than she'd ever felt it before, and so was hers. She'd been wrong to turn him away. He was the only person who could make her whole, and ease the sorrow and anger that had taken up residence inside of her. Her mouth opened to his invasion, she welcomed him with a faint moan as her hands clenched upon his back.

The kiss became more frantic, more desperate. His muscles stood out clearly in his forearms as they quivered around her. His fangs elongated and pressed against her lower lip. Though they were a little uncomfortable, the feel of them caused excitement to spurt through her as she began to tremble. Cassie clung to him, needing something to keep her grounded in the chaos her life had become.

He suddenly pulled away from her, nearly causing her to fall off the bed. His head bowed as his shoulders shook. Cassie knew how he felt as she could barely catch her breath. Her heart pounded rapidly, her body tingled with burning excitement and unfulfilled passion.

"Devon," she ran her hand through his thick black hair as she tried to comfort him.

He shook his head as he moved out of reach. Tears filled her eyes as she recalled all of the problems they'd had before her grandmother died. They had weathered this last storm together, but there was a much larger hurricane still in their way.

She swallowed down the heavy lump lodged in her throat. She couldn't lose him again; she'd just gotten him back. Without him, her life was lost and lonely and full of despair. He was a part of her, and being near her was distressing for him. Cassie hugged herself again as he rose to his feet and strode with easy grace back to her bureau.

Grabbing hold of the tray, he turned back to her again. A muscle in his cheek jumped but he seemed determined to stay near her as he approached again. "It might be easier if you sit in the chair."

Cassie shook her head; her stomach was too upset to put food in it right now. "I'm not hungry."

The muscle in his cheek jumped more forcefully. "You must eat; you have to start taking care of yourself."

"Devon..."

"When was the last time you ate?" he demanded.

Cassie opened her mouth to answer, but closed it again. Her forehead furrowed as she tried to recall the last time she'd eaten a full meal. The fact the answer eluded her was more than a little troubling. She hadn't been hungry lately; she'd been too angry to be hungry, but surely she'd eaten at some point in time. She would have had to, wouldn't she?

Shaking her head, Cassie tried to clear it of her troubling thoughts. She must have snacked at least, but she really couldn't remember when. "I don't know," she admitted reluctantly. The tension in him notched up a level as his eyes scanned her face. "What's wrong?"

He shook his head. "Nothing," he mumbled. "Come on, sit in the chair."

She really didn't feel like eating, but she thought he might force feed her if she didn't try. Deciding to heed his words, she slid from the bed and plodded over to her armchair in the corner. He placed the tray in her lap and pulled the cover off the plate of food. She frowned down at the toast and oatmeal.

"Your stomach probably couldn't handle a big meal right

now," he explained.

Cassie managed a feeble smile. She lifted the spoon and started on the oatmeal. She was surprised by how good it tasted, but she couldn't work up an appetite. "Are you going to watch me the whole time?" she asked as she picked at a piece of toast.

He eyed her warily for a few seconds. "I could use a shower."

Cassie smiled at him and waved her hand toward the bathroom. "Go on, I promise I'll eat it all, but you're making me nervous."

He managed a small grin before nodding to her. Turning away, he went into the bathroom and shut the door. Cassie ate at a snail's pace as she listened to the water. She wasn't fooled into thinking he would be in there for long. Focusing her attention on the oatmeal, she forced more of it down. It wasn't until the shower turned off that she realized the rest of the house was oddly quiet. Where were Chris, Dani, and Melissa? They had been her constant shadows for the past two weeks, but she could hear nothing beyond Devon's shuffling around.

The bathroom door opened and Devon's head popped out. His black hair was tussled and damp as it curled boyishly across his forehead. His eyes focused on her half eaten oatmeal. Cassie's mouth went dry and parted slightly; her eyes almost bulged out of her head as he stepped out of the bathroom.

He hadn't placed his shirt back on, the rigid muscles of his chest, and the ridged lines of his abdomen were clearly revealed to her. His skin was still damp, the glistening water only served to emphasize the carved muscles running through him. Her heart turned over as her toes curled.

Her forgotten spoon hung limply in her hand. Despite the intimacies they had shared, she'd never seen him without his shirt on. Now, she never wanted to see him with it on again.

Taking a deep breath, Cassie raised her gaze to find his emerald eyes watching her keenly. An answering spark of hunger glimmered from him as his full mouth compressed into a line.

She dropped her spoon; she wouldn't get another bite into her, not now. Lowering her gaze to the tray, she was annoyed by the heat burning through her cheeks and creeping down her neck. She had been gaping at him like an idiot, completely revealing her inadequacy around the male form, around *his* form. She had always been a little embarrassed by her lack of experience around him, now she was *mortified*. He must think she was an idiot.

"I'm done," she managed to choke out.

"Maybe you should eat more." She shook her head, unable to meet his gaze again. "Cassie..."

"I'm good," she interrupted. Her mind flashed to Isla, beautiful, seductive, *knowledgeable* Isla. She wouldn't have blushed at the sight of Devon's chest. Isla had seen far more of him, and Cassie was certain Isla hadn't been at all bashful about it. Though she knew Devon had never loved Isla, at one time she had been exactly the type of woman he liked. A type that was *nothing* like her.

She heard him moving around, and then he was taking the tray from her hands. Her face flamed hotter as she saw he'd put his shirt back on. She truly was an idiot, she thought with an inward groan, an immature, foolish, idiot.

He placed the tray back on the bureau and returned to her. Taking hold of her hands he knelt before her again. "I didn't mean to make you uncomfortable."

She glanced at him from under lowered lids. She fought not to blush more, but failed miserably. "You didn't make me uncomfortable."

It wasn't a lie, he hadn't made her uncomfortable. He'd made her many things, but uncomfortable wasn't one of them. He leaned in closer, looking charmingly boyish and hopeful as he peered up at her. She couldn't help but smile at him. She had missed him so much, ached for him every day, and yet she had turned him away. What had she been thinking?

She'd been stricken with grief, but it wasn't an excuse.

"You look exhausted," he said as he brushed back a strand of her hair.

Cassie shrugged absently as she fiddled with the pleat in the workout pants she wore to bed. "Maybe a little," she whispered.

"When was the last time you slept?"

Why did he keep asking her difficult questions? "I've slept here and there," she hedged.

"You ought to sleep."

"The nightmares." She was haunted by the horrifying images of what her grandmother's last moments must have been like.

"I'll keep the nightmares at bay."

Cassie's eyes filled with tears as she caressed his cheek, she loved the feel of his skin beneath her palm. She managed a tremulous smile, she couldn't hurt his feelings, but she was doubtful he could actually keep them away. "Ok."

He took hold of her hands and helped her to her feet. Cassie was surprised by the relief filling her as she climbed onto her bed and curled up beneath the comforters he draped over her. The pillow felt like heaven, the sheets were deliciously smooth against her skin. Devon closed the door, turned off the lamp, and crawled into bed beside her.

His strong arms enveloped her as he pulled her back against his chest. She had forgotten just how right it felt to have him curled up against her, making her feel safe and loved. Her eyes drifted closed as the tranquility settling over her lulled her to sleep.

CHAPTER SIX

CASSIE BLINKED against the rays filtering through the blinds of her windows. It had been a while since she hadn't watched the sun rise. She didn't recall falling asleep, but she must have, and apparently she'd slept through the entire night, without nightmares.

She didn't feel completely rested, but she definitely felt better. She also found a bit of peace for the first time in weeks. Tears of relief and heartache choked her as they fell down her cheeks to wet her pillow. Devon drew her closer as he nuzzled her hair.

"Don't cry love."

His words only made her cry harder. He kissed her cheek as he wiped away her tears with the pad of his thumb. Cassie rolled over to face him and buried her face in his shoulder as she wrapped her arms around him.

Gradually her tears subsided. She was beginning to worry they would never completely subside, at least not for a little while. Not until she truly grieved for her grandmother. Pulling back, she looked up into Devon's much loved face. His jaw was tense, a muscle twitched in his cheek. There was a flat, distant look in his eyes she knew well.

"You should feed," she remarked.

He managed a brief nod; she could hear his teeth grinding. Being this close to her was torture for him when he'd gone awhile without feeding, and he'd been so busy taking care of her last night he hadn't taken care of himself. As she studied him, a consuming need began to build inside of her.

"What about me?"

He blinked as he recoiled from her. "Cassie..."

"You can feed from me Devon."

"No!" He retreated further from her, but she could see the rapidly building hunger flaming through his eyes. He craved this as badly as she did, he was just being stubborn.

"It's ok Devon, you won't hurt me."

Rapidly moving away, he swung his legs over the side of the bed. His hands gripped the mattress so intensely the muscles in his arms stood out. His back was ramrod straight, but a small tremor shook him. Cassie touched his back, but he pulled away and she thought he was going to bolt.

"You won't hurt me," she said again.

He swung toward her, his eyes flashed from their beautiful emerald to a blood red that robbed her of her breath. "You don't know that!" he snarled.

Though he caused her heartbeat to speed up, the trepidation trickling through her was brief. "I do."

He shuddered again. "Cassie your blood, it's a temptation, I'm not sure I can refuse."

"You *can*," she said forcefully. "I want to take care of you like you take care of me. I want to know what *you* feel like."

He shuddered again, and she thought he was going to rip her

mattress apart. She could almost hear his teeth grinding. Cassie sat up and pushed her blankets aside. She rubbed her hands over his rigid back. Though he stiffened, he didn't move away from her as she had feared. He was fighting with himself, but it was a losing battle.

"Cassie," he moaned.

"It's ok," she whispered. "I'm here and I'm willing. It's ok."

He finally turned to her; his gaze searched her face as he looked for any hint she didn't truly want this. "If I hurt you..."

"You won't."

A muscle twitched in his cheek, Cassie soothed it with her hand and pressed her forehead against his. "You're wounded now."

"And you've helped to heal me," she told him.

"Weakened."

She managed a small smile. "Not so much anymore, and I am still stronger than any human."

"If I lose control..."

"You won't."

She wrapped her hand around the back of his neck and kissed him tenderly. He remained rigid against her. She felt a brief tug of guilt, this was torture for him, but if she could ease his thirst she was going to do so. She yearned to be the one he turned to, and she desperately longed to know what it would feel like.

She was surprised the thought didn't repulse her more. Before she'd met him it would have revolted her completely, but now it thrilled and emboldened her. With him, it would be amazing. She was certain of that, even though she had no reason to believe it would be. Everything she'd seen of vampires feeding was gross, brutal, and deadly.

It wouldn't be so now.

Though he still didn't move against her, she felt a yielding in his body. Then, suddenly, his arm snaked around her and locked her into place as his mouth became pliant and demanding against hers. Cassie's heart hammered, her fingers tangled in his hair as he pressed closer against her. A gasp escaped her when he lifted her and laid her on the bed. He pulled back, his eyes questioning and hesitant but simmering with fiery longing. She managed a small nod and a smile.

When he came back to her this time, his kiss wasn't wild with urgency, but so sweet and tender it nearly broke her heart. Cassie savored the delicious sensations he aroused in her body, losing herself to him completely as he kissed her with leisurely thrusts of his tongue. His hands skimmed over her body before settling on either side of her head where he held her as he stroked her face and hair.

Little by little it began to change as his kisses became deeper and his body became more rigid against her. She didn't know when he'd last fed, but she suspected he hadn't been doing it as often as he should, and that was her fault. He'd been so busy watching over her, he hadn't been taking care of himself. Guilt tugged at Cassie as she became desperate to be the one to ease his torment.

Grasping his head, Cassie knew she would have to make the first move. He wouldn't go any further otherwise. Gently guiding his head down, she turned her head to allow him better access to her neck. His mouth was hot on her skin as his body became immobile against hers once more. Cassie's heart thumped loudly, each pulse was like a drumbeat in her ears.

She waited breathlessly as with a small moan, he brushed his lips against the tender skin of her neck. Cassie's hands tensed in his hair as she felt the fluttering brush of his fangs, and then he struck.

Cassie arched off the bed, a small breath escaped as her. His hand entangled in her hair, pulling her head back he sank deeper into her to drink in deep, greedy gulps. Cassie turned her head to the side as the pain faded away and pleasure rushed forward to engulf her in waves that left her breathless and limp. Her grip eased on him as she became suffused in a world of ecstasy and pleasure.

It took her a moment to realize it was his pleasure she felt. It wrapped her within a cocoon of warmth. His love was so true, so pure it robbed her of all logical thought. It ended all her doubts, and any self-consciousness she'd ever experienced in his presence.

She suddenly saw herself through his eyes, and to him she was beautiful, loving and strong. He knew she wasn't perfect, and he loved her more for her faults. There was nothing about her he would change. Tears burned her eyes as her heart swelled to the point where she thought it would burst.

She could also feel the thirst constantly pulling at him. The battle he fought within himself every moment of every day, especially around her, to retain control of his murderous instincts was staggering. The control it took for him to be around her was far more than she ever could have imagined, and she loved him more for his ability to do so.

Cassie tried desperately to reciprocate her own pleasure and love to him, praying fervently he would feel it as clearly as she felt his. She cradled him against her, unaware of the tears of joy and love sliding down her face. "I love you," she whispered over and over, just in case her thoughts weren't reaching him.

When he bit deeper she felt no concern. She simply allowed herself to drift inside of his love, gratification, and delight. Though she knew he could kill her, this bond was so intimate and breathtaking she never wanted it to stop.

He broke away suddenly; his body shook, his head dropped onto her shoulder. Though he wasn't feeding upon her, she was surprised to realize the bond hadn't been broken. His emotions still thrummed against her, his love still enveloped her.

"I'm fine," she assured him. He lifted his head and turned toward her. His eyes gleamed as he tried to assure himself she wasn't lying to him. More power than she had ever seen radiated from him. Satisfaction and pleasure filled her at the realization it was *her* blood that had caused the influx of strength in him. "Did you take enough?"

He bent his forehead to hers. "Plenty," he whispered hoarsely. "Are you sure you're ok?"

Cassie slid her fingers over his beloved face. "I am so much better than just ok."

Seeming to finally believe her, he rolled to the side and drew her against him. Cassie sighed contentedly as she rested her hand on his chest. He rubbed her back as he idly played with her hair. "That was amazing," she murmured, her eyes drifted closed as serenity enshrouded her.

"It was."

Cassie yawned and burrowed herself against his side. "Is it always like that? Can you always feel other people's emotions?"

"We can keep people shut out if we choose, but the exchange of blood opens the pathway between the two minds."

"Do you always let people in?"

"Not in a while. I never cared what anyone felt when I thought it might be pleasurable for them. But sometimes..." he broke off, seemingly hesitant to continue on, but he did. "Sometimes I enjoyed feeling the anguish."

"Is it painful to some for long?" she whispered.

His body became taut against her, not liking this line of

questioning, but he wouldn't keep anything from her. "It can be," he admitted.

She shuddered as thoughts of her grandmother blazed into her mind, but she quickly shut them down. This was only about the two of them, she wasn't going to let the outside world intrude upon the ecstasy she'd found here, no matter how brief it might be.

"Why wasn't it for me?"

His lips were warm against her temple and ear as he turned into her. Though his body temperature was lower than hers, he never failed to heat her. "Because you were willing. It's painful if you fight against it, which most people do, but if you are willing... things are different if you give your blood freely."

Cassie yawned again, her hand curled into his shirt over the place where his still heart was nestled. His hand curled up the back of her head to cup her as he dropped a kiss on her brow. "I have never experienced that before."

Cassie's head shot up. She didn't like to think about all of the many women he had shared blood with over the years, especially not Isla. "Really?"

He smiled at her as his fingers trailed over her shoulder. "Really."

She frowned at him. "How is that possible?"

"I've never met a willing human before, and I've never exchanged blood with a vampire."

"Why not?"

His hand stilled on her shoulder as his eyes burned into hers. "When vampires exchange blood with each other, the pathways open more. It is a very intimate thing, one only certain vampires share with each other and one I never wished to share with someone else, until now."

Cassie couldn't stop the goofy grin spreading over her face

at his words. She couldn't deny the thrill of possession and supe-
riority tearing through her. They finally had one thing that was
theirs. He grinned back at her and pulled her down to kiss her
lovingly. She was just beginning to lose herself in his kiss when
he pulled away, dropped a chaste kiss on her nose and pulled her
head down against his shoulder. "Rest."

She wanted to protest his gruff order, but his body was
unyielding against hers. It was taking all he had to keep himself
away from her. Plus, it was difficult to argue when her eyelids
were drifting closed and her body settled against his.

CHAPTER SEVEN

DEVON THREW the door of the bathroom open and winced as it rebounded off the wall. He still wasn't used to the strength of Cassie's blood inside of him. In all of his hundreds of years, and thousands of victims, he had never tasted anything, or experienced anything, as delicious and potent as she was.

It was more than just the power inside of her, and the thrill she gave to him. It was also her openness; her trust and unadulterated love for him that made him feel as if he could take on the world. He could do anything with her at his side, and he hoped one day she would choose to stay by his side forever.

Though they hadn't discussed it again, it was something they would have to confront sooner rather than later. Tasting her today had eased the fiery appetite of the beast inside him, but she was still human, and that was the biggest problem. He wanted her to be safe from the world of death she resided in.

He knew she was his mate. It was a rare thing for a vampire to find, but once mates were discovered they could never be separated. If she had continued to rebuff him, he would have let her be, but eventually it would have destroyed him. He couldn't be certain he wouldn't have come back for her anyway.

He wasn't willing to tell her about being mates yet. He desired her to change because she wanted to be with him for eternity, and not because she felt obligated in order to keep him stable and happy. He was also afraid of what may reside within her, and the distinct possibility he may never be able to change her.

Her head turned toward him as he emerged and her shoulders slumped. A blanket was wrapped around her shoulders and her golden hair cascaded around her in disheveled curls. Her face had been ashen, but color flooded into it the minute she saw him. "Are you hungry?" he inquired as he glanced at the clock. It was almost eight; she'd slept most of the day away.

"Famished," she admitted.

He smiled as he moved toward her. "Let's get you some food."

Taking hold of her hand, he helped her to her feet. He searched her face for any sign he'd injured her in any way. He'd taken more blood than he should have, more than he had intended, but she'd tasted so good, and been so willing that he'd become lost in her. Her love had ensnared him in a web he'd feared he wouldn't be able to break free from. But he'd controlled himself far better than he'd thought he could. He was beginning to realize that when it came to her, he was able to do almost anything.

"Are you feeling ok?"

She glanced up at him from under her sweeping dark lashes. "I feel perfectly fine. Stop worrying so much." Pulling the blanket from her shoulders she dropped it on the bed. "Is everyone else downstairs?"

"Yes." A troubled look crossed her delicate features. "What's wrong?"

She shook her head as she flashed him a fleeting grin. "I just hope they're not mad at me."

"Of course they're not."

"I treated them badly."

"They understand Cassie."

"I hope so."

She moved past him and gathered clothes before disappearing into the bathroom. Waiting patiently he sat on the edge of the bed until she returned. The black turtleneck she wore highlighted her creamy complexion and golden hair, while clinging to her lithe figure. He marveled at her beauty as she moved gracefully across the room and grabbed her hair brush.

He rose and came up behind her as she finished brushing her hair. Her eyes caught his in the mirror, a small smile played across her full mouth. He pulled down the collar of her turtleneck, his body tightened at the sight of the two marks on her neck. *His* marks.

A thrill of possession raced through him. She was his completely, and always, even if he couldn't change her. She flinched briefly as he rested his fingertips against them. "I can get rid of those for you," he murmured.

He should have done it to begin with, but he had liked the idea of her bearing his mark. But now that she was going back into the world, it would be safer for all of them if he closed the wounds.

Cassie rested her hand over his. "That's ok, I like knowing they're there, and they probably won't last. I heal..."

"Fast," he finished for her, hating the reminder of the frightening abilities she possessed.

She smiled innocently at him in the mirror; she had no idea

the direction his thoughts had taken. He shuddered as he fought the consuming urge to pull her against him and never leave this room. She turned into him, and wrapping her arms around his waist she rested her head against his chest. His fingers entangled in her silken hair as he held her against him.

All of the torment he had been living with for the past couple of weeks was gone. She calmed every ragged piece of his soul. The rumbling of her stomach brought him back to reality. Releasing her, he pulled the turtleneck up and covered the bite. She smiled up at him as her fingers easily slid into his. She fidgeted with the collar of her shirt as they left the room. He leaned close enough that his lips brushed against her cheek. "It will be ok."

Hushed voices drifted from the kitchen, and the scraping of silverware on plates could be heard. Cassie nervously glanced up at him as he stepped through the door, and pulled her behind him. She stood half behind him as a small tremor shook her hand.

Chris, Melissa, and Dani looked up as they entered. Worry flashed briefly across their faces as they glanced from Devon to Cassie. Chris's eyes remained locked on Devon's before he turned his attention to Cassie. She managed a wan smile for them as her fingers fiddled with her shirt once more.

"Hi guys," she greeted.

"How are you feeling?" Melissa inquired anxiously.

"Much better."

Chris rose and strode across the room to her. "It's good to have you back."

He enfolded her in a bear hug as he lifted her up. Devon felt Cassie's jolt of surprise before she wrapped her arms around him. Devon fought the jealousy and possessive urge coursing through him as Chris swung her back and forth, shaking her legs in the air until she laughed. Chris was her best friend, he knew that. Hell, he was Devon's best friend now, but he still didn't like other men touching her.

Cassie beamed up at Chris as he dropped her down and took a step back. "It's good to be back."

"You're feeling better?"

"Yes, I'm sorry for the way I've acted," her gaze flitted to Dani and Melissa. "To all of you."

Melissa was grinning from ear to ear as she hurried over to hug Cassie. "It's ok, we understand. I'm just so happy you're back."

Tears shimmered in Cassie's eyes as Melissa took a step away and Dani embraced her. "Are you hungry?" Chris asked anxiously. "Melissa made baked ziti, and I have to admit it's not half bad."

Melissa shoved his shoulder. "Not half bad? You're on your third helping."

He grinned back at her, before turning on his heel and hurrying to grab a plate. Cassie took hold of Devon's hand again as she made her way to the island everyone had gathered around. Chris slapped an overflowing plate of food in front of her. "You've got a lot of catching up to do," he explained.

Cassie laughed as she picked up her fork and dug in. Devon watched her carefully, relieved to see her eating with such gusto, and that he hadn't taken too much blood. He had planned to give her a little of his blood, not enough to change her, but enough to give her some strength after the blood loss she'd experienced.

However, he'd decided against it almost immediately. He wanted her to have his blood inside her, and to know what it would be like to have her feeding from him. But he couldn't take the risk something might happen to her if he did give her his blood. Not when he and Luther still had no idea exactly what Cassie was.

~

"APPARENTLY THEY WEREN'T BEING indifferent to me because of my grandmother's death, but because I had stopped dating you."

Cassie glanced up at Devon who rigidly stood behind her in the lunch line. His hand tightened on her waist as his gaze disdainfully raked the cafeteria. The buzz about her, which had died down after her grandmother's death, had now returned tenfold. The nasty whispers were rapidly flying around, the irate glares and waves of hatred were once more pounding against her. Though she had tried to become accustomed to it all, she still didn't like it, or understand it. She knew the girls desired Devon, but so much hatred because of jealousy was something she would never understand.

His mouth was warm as he kissed her neck through the material of her dark green turtleneck. Cassie pressed closer as her toes curled and her breath hitched. He nudged her forward as the line moved. She made a face over being interrupted but grabbed a tray. She was grateful Devon was with her. None of the girls would dare be catty or cruel to her in front of him, and after Devon had lifted Mark with one hand and slammed him into a wall, none of the boys were willing to risk having his wrath and strength turned on them either. His presence also helped to keep her stable and grounded, helped to ease the sting the cruel comments inflicted.

Reaching the front of the line, Cassie grabbed her food, paid for it, and hurried free of the confining lunch line. Dani and Chris were already at the table. Cassie slouched into her chair and took a deep breath of relief. "How's it going?" Chris inquired.

"Just peachy," she replied but she managed a wry smile.

Chris's eyes were troubled as he scanned the cafeteria. "Bunch of jerks," he mumbled.

"I'm used to it by now."

Melissa dropped her lunch bag on the table, slid into her chair and dug out an apple. "What an awful day," she muttered.

"I second that," Chris agreed.

Cassie shrugged as her gaze fell on Devon. He was back in her life now, so no matter how bad the day was it could never be as terrible as the past couple of weeks. Her fingers flitted up to her neck. Though she was a fast healer, the marks were still barely visible upon her skin. Touching them now, she was once more swept away by the rush of love that had encompassed her when he'd been feeding upon her.

Cassie didn't realize she had stopped breathing until he sat back. "Eat," he whispered.

She lifted her pizza up and began to pick at her food. "When is Luther coming back?" Chris inquired.

Melissa shrugged as she eyed her sandwich with a curved upper lip. "I don't know, I haven't heard from him in a couple of days." Devon shifted beside her, his hand idly rubbed the back of her neck. Though he appeared nonchalant she sensed a sudden tension humming through him. "Probably soon."

Cassie forced herself to swallow the soggy pizza. "You know we should probably go out hunting tonight."

Devon's hand momentarily constricted on the back of her neck. "Cassie..."

"We *have* to go back out," she insisted. "They're still out there. They're going to start killing people again. I just wish I knew where they've been hiding out." That was the worst of it, she knew they were out there, but they had been laying low for so long she was becoming truly apprehensive about what they were planning. Devon began to caress her again when she shuddered with dread. "Do you know where they are?"

Devon's dark hair fell across his forehead as he shook his head. "No, Cassie."

"But they are planning something big?"

His forehead furrowed. "I don't know what they're planning Cass, but I don't think it's a good idea for you to go back out there right now."

Her eyes narrowed. "I'm much better now."

"But you're still angry and..."

"Of course I'm angry," she interrupted hotly. Taking a deep breath she forced herself to remain calm, being flustered and bitter would get her nowhere. "But something has to be done before they destroy more families."

Devon's shoulders sagged. "I know how you feel Cassie, but why don't you wait until Luther comes back?"

"Why? We've gone out since he left."

"I know that, but I still think it would be best if you waited. Give yourself a little more time to regroup, and Luther is your Guardian."

She glanced around the cafeteria as she took in all the people who had turned against her. Though they hated her now, the last thing she wanted was for one of them to experience the heart wrenching loss she felt. They may hate her, but she was the only protection they had against the monsters stalking their town, and she was going to do everything she could to keep them safe.

Swirling flakes of snow spiraled lazily outside the cafeteria windows. "Why have they been so quiet?" she whispered thoughtfully. Out of the corner of her eye she caught the fleeting glances they all exchanged. "What's with the look?"

Melissa placed her tomato sandwich down and leaned back in her chair. Her onyx eyes gleamed in the harsh radiance of the cafeteria. "They haven't," she answered.

"Excuse me?" Cassie asked.

"They haven't been quiet," Chris said more forcefully. "They are out there."

"I don't understand what you're saying; no murders have been reported..."

"Cassie, when was the last time you read the paper or watched the news?"

Her hands fisted, her eyes flickered to Devon who was watching her intently. Swallowing heavily, she turned her attention back to Chris. "I... I don't know," she reluctantly admitted.

"They have been out there Cass. There have been murders, or animal attacks, or whatever the police are coming up with to help them sleep at night. There have been more missing people reported."

"Why didn't you tell me?"

They all shifted uncomfortably as they glanced at each other. Chris leaned across the table and rested his hand on hers. "Because we didn't think you could handle it."

"Yes, I could have!" she retorted.

"Cassie, you could barely handle crawling out of bed in the morning."

Tears burned the back of her eyes; guilt filled her as she shook her head. She tried to deny his words, but she *knew* they were right. She was an idiot, she realized with a silent groan. She should have known Julian and Isla wouldn't go into hiding, especially not after the blow they'd dealt to her. They would be relishing in their victory over her, and reveling in her inability to stop them. Her failure to handle her grief and anger had caused more people to be killed. Guilt and self-hatred nearly choked her with their intensity.

"It's my fault then."

"Of course not," Devon responded as he shot Chris an irritated look. "You're human Cassie, you lost a loved one and you had to grieve. It's Julian and Isla's fault, not yours."

Cassie turned away from him, it didn't matter what he said she was going to blame herself. "But I'm not human," she lamented. "So that's more of a reason to get out there in force now."

"We'll figure it out Cassie."

She frowned at him, but nodded just to keep him satisfied. The snow outside began to swirl more rapidly as the wind howled against the glass. Cassie shivered in response and huddled deeper into her turtleneck and sweater. The sky was an oppressive steel gray that hung heavy in the air.

Cassie searched the dark day as she recalled the cloudy day on the beach when they'd first felt Julian's twisted presence. It had been overcast, making it possible for him to move about in the daytime, much like today. A knot twisted in Cassie's stomach, a feeling of foreboding raced down her spine.

Glancing around the cafeteria, she briefly envied everyone their simple, ignorant lives. They had no idea what lurked out there, what hunted them, what cruelty resided in the world. They knew football games, dances, and parties. It was a simple life, one she should have had, but was glad she didn't.

For every twist and turn in her life had brought her to Devon, and there was nothing she would change about that outcome.

"They're planning something bad," she whispered.

"Do you have premonitions now too?" Chris inquired.

Cassie forced a smile to her lips. "No, just a feeling."

She pushed her plate away as she gave up on eating anymore. The knot in her stomach killed her appetite completely. Devon took hold of her hand and began to massage the back of it with his thumb, and Cassie lost herself to the comfort of his touch.

CHAPTER EIGHT

THE SNOW still fell in lazy spirals that had piled up on the lawn, and coated the trees. Cassie turned away from the window, happy to be inside and out of the cold. Chris, Dani, and Melissa were gathered around the island, talking as they dealt another hand of cards. A twinge tugged at Cassie's heart, her grandmother had loved to play cards. They used to have nights where they would all sit and play together. Unfortunately, those nights had been few and far between before her grandmother had passed on.

Pouring a cup of coffee she blew on it before taking a sip. Devon strode into the room. Her heart flipped in her chest, her stomach did a strange turn. His eyes instantly found hers and a beautiful grin spread over his full lips. His hair, still damp from his shower, was tussled across his forehead. She smiled at him, and turned her attention back to her coffee, before memories of the intimacy of last night took over. Absently, she touched the marks on her neck as she recalled him there, gaining strength from her body.

"Still snowing?" His solid legs brushed against hers as he stopped before her and leaned forward to push aside the curtain. Cassie's mouth went dry; her body instinctively pressed closer to his as need ensnared her. The enticing blend of soap and spices he emitted caused her hands to tighten on her mug.

She tilted her head back to look at him, not at all surprised to find his eyes on her. Leaning closer, he rested his hands against the counter on either side of her. There were other people in the room, but she couldn't bring herself to care as every cell inside her became focused upon him.

"Like crazy. Maybe we won't have school tomorrow," Dani said cheerfully.

"Hmm," Chris absently agreed.

Cassie barely heard their conversation over the excitement pounding through her. Something inside of her was shifting, changing, growing. She was beginning to realize it was only a matter of time before she lost complete control, and allowed free rein to everything she was thinking and feeling.

She'd thought she would be frightened by that realization, she wasn't. She was actually thrilled and awed by it. Things were going to change drastically between them, and she was eager to embrace *every* one of those changes.

Cassie started in surprise when Devon's phone went off and he pulled it out of his pocket. Worry flashed through his eyes as he read the message, hit a few buttons and put it back in his pocket. His eyes were cold and distant when they came back to hers. "Who... who was that?" She had to fight to keep the nervousness from her voice.

"I have to go out for a bit."

"Out? Where?" Unreasonable panic filled her; she couldn't understand the abrupt change that had come over him. Moments ago he'd been warm and caring, now he was a stranger. She didn't know who he could be talking to that would cause such a change. Almost everyone he talked to was in this room, unless it was a girl. Cassie quickly shut the thought down. She'd experienced his feelings last night and she knew he only thought of her, only loved her. But who could he possibly have been talking to?

"I just need to pick up a few things from my place."

"Can you grab me some things too?" Chris asked absently.

Cassie felt her mouth drop as she turned toward Chris. Chris froze, his hands tensed around the cards he held as he realized exactly what it was he had let slip out. "Too?" she inquired softly.

Chris's eyes darted to Devon. "Chris has been staying at my place every once in a while," Devon answered as he rested his hands on her shoulders.

Betrayal flared inside her, but she somehow managed to push it back before it consumed her again. She knew how awful Chris's home life was. Her grandmother had taken care of him more than his own mother had, and he had spent most of his nights sleeping on Cassie's floor. It would have been difficult for him to be here after her grandmother had died, and Cassie understood that, but she couldn't shake the shock that kept her riveted.

Just how close had they gotten over the past two weeks?

"I see," she murmured.

"Cassie..."

"No, it's fine. I'm fine, really." She cut Chris off as she forced a reassuring smile. "Really."

"I'm sorry I didn't tell you," Chris said. "I just... I just needed a break."

"A break?"

His smile was feeble as he ducked his head. "Your emotions,

and Devon's, weren't exactly easy to deal with, and I couldn't keep them shut out."

"Oh," Cassie said dully. If Devon was here watching over her, Chris would have been bombarded with both of their emotions, even at his own house. Devon firmly folded his arms over his chest. He didn't look comfortable with the issue of his emotions being spoken about so freely. "Sorry."

Chris grinned at her. "It's quite alright, the giant TV more than made up for not being able to stay at my own crappy house."

Cassie blinked in surprise then glanced questioningly at Devon. "Not mine," he said with a casual shrug. "I have to go, but I'll be back in a little bit."

He bent to drop a quick kiss on her cheek. Cassie's hand lingered on his face as she traced its much loved contours. She had a bad feeling about him leaving, but she couldn't appear to be a clingy girlfriend. "Be safe."

A grin teased the corners of his mouth. "Stay inside."

"Oh you can count on that," Melissa said as she shivered. "Damn weather."

Devon kissed her again and squeezed her hand before leaving the room. Cassie turned back to the window to watch as he hurried to his car. He was huddled into his jacket with his hands shoved into his pockets. An ache bloomed in her chest. Shaking her head, she turned away from the window. She was being ridiculous; he would only be gone for a little while.

However, they had spent too much time apart, and she had only recently gotten him back in her life. She wasn't ready to be separated from him now. Cassie rubbed the bridge of her nose as she stepped away from the counter. Chris tapped the stool beside him for her to sit down.

"I'll deal you in."

"Sounds good," she mumbled.

❧

DEVON PULLED his car into Luther's driveway and shut the car off. He wasn't sure he was ready to know what Luther had learned, if anything. Luther's text had simply said he had to speak with him as soon as possible. That didn't mean Luther had learned something, he may simply aim to speak with Devon when no one else was around. Luther didn't know Cassie was with him again and doing better now.

All of that might be about to change.

Devon pushed his car door open. It couldn't be avoided; he had to know what had happened while Luther was gone. Trudging through the snow, he dreaded every step he took. He was almost to the door when Luther opened it.

Luther's normally neat hair was in disarray. The fine lines around his mouth and eyes were drawn and pinched. His glasses were already in hand. One look at him told Devon he wasn't going to like what the man had to say.

It wasn't the cold of the night causing the chill in him now. "You learned something," he said flatly.

Luther slid his glasses back on and nodded briskly. "I did. You had better come in."

Stepping inside, he waited as Luther closed the door behind him and shut out the storm. Devon followed as Luther moved into the living room. Neither of them sat as Luther began to pace. "Is it what I feared?" Devon inquired.

Luther pulled his glasses off again and squeezed his nose with his fingers. "I think it may be worse."

Devon felt as if someone had socked him in the stomach. Terror permeated him; his hands fisted at his sides. He was prepared to fight for Cassie, prepared to die for her, but he couldn't defend her from herself.

~

"WHAT WAS THAT?"

Cassie lowered her cards as she strained to see or hear what had caught Dani's attention. Dani was standing by the backdoor with the light on as she watched the snow. "What was what?" Chris asked around a mouthful of chips.

"I thought I saw something." A shiver raced down Cassie's back as foreboding crept into her stomach. Dani took a small step back from the door and glanced at them. "I *know* I saw something," she whispered.

The lights flickered out. Cassie nearly knocked her water over as she bumped the table. She righted it quickly as the lights flickered back on and then flickered out again. Cassie rose and strode purposely to the back door. "Cassie," Chris warned.

"I'm not going out there," she assured him.

Dani pointed toward the thick copse of oak trees at the edge of the backyard, just beyond her old tire swing. Narrowing her eyes, Cassie focused all of her attention there. Then she saw it, a flash of movement to the right that snapped her head in that direction. Dani bumped into Cassie as she took a frightened step back. Chris and Melissa were already on their feet; their eyes round as they edged closer.

"Go," Cassie urged away from the threshold as she nudged her back toward the house.

She had a bad feeling she already knew who was out there, and she didn't intend for Dani to go anywhere near them. Glancing back, she froze as ice crept through her veins. Her hand squeezed on Dani's shoulder, unintentionally holding her in place as her legs became blocks of cement. Isla had appeared in the backyard, her auburn hair was coated with flakes of falling snow. The low cut black dress she wore hugged her curvaceous figure as the bottom of it floated about her in the wind.

However, it was not the haunting beauty of the woman, or her sudden appearance that made Cassie freeze instantly. No, it was the person by her side. The boy's brunette hair stood out in sharp contrast to the snow as it tumbled around him in wet straggles. Snow was beginning to turn his hair a grayish brown color. The boy was young, no more than twelve or thirteen.

Nausea curdled in Cassie's stomach, a lump lodged in her throat as Dani took a step closer to her. Cassie didn't know what to do as Chris and Melissa moved closer. Isla flashed a smile at them, and flicked the snow off of her as she shook back her dark hair. With a crooked finger she beckoned tauntingly for them to come outside. "What do we do?" Dani whispered.

Isla lifted the boy from the ground and lifted him off his feet by the back of his shirt. Blood trickled down his neck to stain the thin shirt he wore. Melissa gasped, while Dani let out a low moan. "We go out there," Cassie answered.

"Cassie..."

"We have to Melissa. We *have* to."

Melissa sighed before nodding her agreement. "I know, but I think we should prepare a little first."

Cassie nervously bit on her bottom lip as she studied the swirling snow. Aside from Isla the scene was blessedly, deceivingly tranquil. It should be a fiery scene from Hell out there, or at least thunder and lightning, instead of the beautiful wonderland surrounding the monster in her backyard.

But no matter how surreal it all was, Cassie knew they had

to go out there and face it. That *she* had to go out there and face it. "Get the supplies and meet me out there," she instructed.

"Cassie." Chris grabbed hold of her arm. "Melissa and I are coming with you. Dani, in the living room there's a trunk..."

"I know where it is," Dani interrupted.

"Is Julian out there?" Melissa inquired, her eyes focused on Chris.

Chris's gaze became distant as his forehead furrowed. "I don't feel him out there, but it doesn't mean he isn't. He was able to keep himself cloaked from me before. Unless he aspires to let us to know he's there, we won't."

Fear slid through her belly but she abruptly pushed it aside. There was no room for fear here, there never had been. There never would be. "Go Dani," Melissa urged.

She turned to hurry away, but Cassie grabbed hold of her arm, and slipped her cell phone into Dani's hand. "Call Devon," she whispered, hoping Isla couldn't hear her over the rising crescendo of the wind, and the door.

Dani's eyes shimmered with tears before she nodded and fled the room. "Come on," Chris said.

He pulled the door open. Cassie flinched as the sting of the icy wind hit her. The sneakers she slipped on did little to barricade her feet against the snow. It trickled down inside of them and froze against her sockless skin. She wanted to hug herself against the cold, but she didn't dare keep her hands occupied with anything.

Isla smiled at them as she released the young boy. He collapsed into the snow, and barely lifted his head before letting it drop again. Cassie took a step toward him but Chris seized hold of her arm. "Where's your friend?" His voice rose to be heard across the distance.

Isla shrugged a dainty, bared shoulder. She had to be freezing, but she showed no signs of it. "I planned for this to be just the two of us; Julian graciously agreed to it."

The two of us? Cassie's gaze slid to Chris and Melissa as more than just the icy trickle of snow slid down her back. The two of us wouldn't include them.

~

"THAT WAS the most I could find on any of the other Hunters with Cassie's ability, or lack thereof."

Devon stared out the window as Luther finished speaking. His hands clenched and unclenched as his mind raced at a hundred miles an hour. He didn't know what to think about what Luther had just told him. "But you found records of the one Hunter like Cassie dying in a strange manner? Of her acting differently than the others?" he asked.

"Yes, strange behavior was recorded about her before she died, or The Commission killed her."

Devon turned abruptly toward him. "Killed her?" he demanded.

Luther nodded as he rubbed at his temples. "Yes, The Commission wouldn't be willing to admit there was a mistake somewhere in The Hunter bloodline, and they wouldn't let anyone else to know about it. They would make sure it was buried, even if it meant destroying the only piece of evidence there was, the girl herself."

Disgust curdled through Devon's stomach at the thought of the cold hearted bastards who ran The Guardians and The Hunters. At one point, The Commission had consisted of the twelve oldest Guardians, and they had dictated where every Hunter and Guardian would go. Devon had no idea how many of them were left, if any, since The Slaughter. After hearing

Luther's words, he hoped they were all dead, because if they weren't...

If they weren't, they would come for Cassie.

A tremor worked through him, his hands fisted at his sides as he fought the urge to smash the walls. "They destroyed the girl," he growled.

Luther's eyes were sorrowful as he met Devon's gaze. "I believe they did. It was only pure luck I ran across a book with notes from that particular Hunter's Guardian in it. He didn't want her death covered up, he wanted what happened to her to be known, but unfortunately he didn't have a choice."

"The Commission made him cover it up?" Devon inquired.

"I think they killed him too."

Devon's mouth dropped. "What?"

"The girl's name was Gertrude, her Guardian Henry died shortly after she was killed. Both of their deaths were recorded as *means unknown*. After Gertrude there were no more Hunter's like Cassie. For over three hundred years, every Hunter has had some ability. Cassie is the first Hunter not to have one in a *very* long time."

Devon was baffled as he stared at Luther. The Guardians knew how *every* one of their kind had died, along with their Hunters. They kept meticulous notes about it, notes Devon had tediously helped to sift through. Every one of the Hunters and Guardians had been meticulously accounted for from the minute of their birth to the minute of their demise. That this particular Hunter, and Guardian, had somehow slipped through the cracks was a giant red flag something was wrong.

"Does The Commission know you were looking for this information?"

Luther closed his eyes and dropped his head into his hands. "I don't know. I tried to keep the search as quiet as possible, but with everyone as scattered as they are I did have to contact more people than I'd planned on. It was one of these people who allowed me access to his vast collection. The book on Gertrude was buried in his basement, forgotten. I don't think he knew he had it."

"But if he did?"

Luther's hair was in disarray as he continued to tug at it. "I don't consider him close enough to say I trust him."

If Devon still needed to breathe, he knew he wouldn't be able to do so anymore as fear stole it from him. "Does The Commission still exist?" Devon demanded.

"They are not as powerful as before, but yes, they still exist." Luther seemed hesitant to continue. Then, he just plunged on. "Devon, I don't think Gertrude is an isolated incident. I think The Commission may have killed off *all* of the others like Cassie, or at least they did after Gertrude."

"What?" Devon managed to croak out.

"Before Gertrude there was at least one Hunter every few decades with no abilities. After, there were none. I think The Commission began to kill them off in order to limit the liability these Hunters represented to them."

Devon's legs almost buckled, he had to lean against the door jam in order to keep himself upright. "Are you serious?"

Luther pulled his glasses off. "I believe in what I do, Devon. I believe I help in the world, that I am part of a *good* cause. But I am aware The Commission was full of a bunch of old fashioned, uppity individuals who wouldn't allow any imperfection, and to them, these Hunters were a liability. They would worry that whatever happened to Gertrude could happen to Cassie..."

Luther broke off, his unspoken words hung heavily in the air. Devon knew what he'd been unwilling to say though. If The Commission somehow knew what Luther had been digging for, and why he had been digging for it, they might come for Cassie. They wouldn't take any chance there was a fault in what was left of the Hunter bloodline. He had to get Cassie out of this town; there was far too much danger here for her. Unfortunately, leaving was something she absolutely refused to do. Cursing violently, Devon spun and stalked back the other way.

"Cassie is not an imperfection."

Luther nodded as he slid his glasses on. "I know that, but to them she would be. If they thought the other Hunters like her were a threat to The Commission in any way, they would have destroyed them."

Devon was barely able to form a coherent thought. Fury boiled through him at the thought of those men sitting back, idly deciding who would live, and who would die. "So, The Slaughter may very well have saved her life," Devon muttered.

Luther closed his eyes as he inhaled deeply. "As ironic as that is, yes. The Slaughter could be the reason she *is* still alive."

"They'll come for her, if they know what you were looking for, they'll come for her."

"There aren't enough of them left to bother her Devon." Luther didn't sound completely convinced though. "And we don't know if anything will come of what I uncovered."

Devon didn't believe that. "Do we tell her?"

Devon's phone went off; the ringer was loud in the oppressive room. He fished it out of his pocket, his chest constricted at the display of Cassie's name. He didn't know what to say to her right now, he didn't know if he could keep the stress out of his voice. He almost slipped the phone back in his pocket, but she would only worry if he didn't answer, and the last thing he intended was to cause her more stress.

He held up a finger to Luther as he walked a few feet away. "Hello."

"Devon! Devon! You have to get back here as soon as possible! Now!" A voice rushed over the line.

He froze as he tried to place the strange voice on the other end of his phone. "Dani?" he asked in surprise.

"Yes, yes," she replied impatiently. "You need to get back here *now*! Isla's outside, and they're outside with her; I have to go help them!"

Devon stood for a stunned moment after the line went dead. Then panic tore through him. Dropping the phone, he raced past a startled Luther and threw the door open. "Devon!" Luther shouted in surprise.

"Cassie's!" he yelled back at him.

Leaping into the storm, Devon drew on every ounce of power Cassie's blood had given to him as he raced into the night.

No matter how fast he moved, he was terrified he wouldn't get to her in time.

CHAPTER NINE

CASSIE TOOK a protective step closer to Melissa and Chris. Isla hadn't moved yet, but there was a strangely superior smile on her face as in the air Cassie felt a sizzling power beginning to build. Her heart plummeted as she glanced at Chris and Melissa. She belatedly recalled they'd never asked Devon what Isla's power was. The backdoor slammed open a split second before Isla released her power in a brutal rush of electricity.

A crushing jolt seemed to turn the world upside down. Cassie took a deep breath as she tried to ease the accelerated beat of her heart. Her skin tickled strangely, her hair stood on end. She looked down to find the ends of her arm hair were singed. The stench of burnt flesh and hair hung heavy in the damp air.

She spun in a circle when she realized Chris and Melissa weren't standing beside her anymore. Nausea spiraled through her as she raced toward where they lay prone on the ground. "No, no, no!" she cried as she fell to her knees in the snow beside Chris.

Grasping hold of his arm, she was horrified by the burns marring his pale skin. But she felt the reassuring beat of his heart and warmth of his skin. Glancing at Melissa she was relieved to see the subtle rise and fall of her chest.

Dani fell into the snow beside her, her gold flecked eyes were as round as saucers as she gaped at Cassie. Cassie recalled what Devon had said about the abilities of a Grounder. When a vampire and a Hunter met up, they cancelled each other out. That was why Dani was still on her feet, but why was *she*?

Cassie glanced back at Isla. Apparently Isla had more control over who she could and could not take out with her power than Dani did. Cassie shuddered, she had to keep Isla from her friends, but she had no idea how she was going to do it. "You have to get them inside," she whispered to Dani.

Dani's frightened gaze shot to Isla. "I can't leave you out here."

"She won't let me get inside, she *might* let you. You need to get them out of here."

"Cassie..."

Cassie pulled the stake from where it had been tucked into the sleeve of Dani's coat. "Go on."

"But..."

"Dani, the three of you must live through this. You have to help them." Dani's eyes were troubled. "It's me she's after, now go."

Before Dani could protest further, Cassie scuttled back in the snow. She barely felt the cold through the adrenaline coursing in her veins. No matter what happened, she had to keep Isla away from the three of them, but it was going to be a battle unlike any Cassie had ever experienced. One she most likely would not survive.

A brief tug of guilt and loss pulled at her heart as her

thoughts turned to Devon. They had just found each other again, and this was going to destroy him. She shut the thoughts down before she was consumed by the agony trying to rise up. She still had a chance to win this, and she was going to fight like a wildcat to make sure she didn't lose him again.

Cassie turned toward Isla as the beautiful woman sauntered forward with her hips swaying, and her hair falling about her in thick waves. Cassie remained kneeling, her body tense as she tried to calculate Isla's plan. Her fingers tightened around the stake as Isla stopped mere feet away from her, and her golden eyes narrowed as she studied Cassie distastefully.

"What could Devon possibly see in you?" she mused as she tapped her teeth with a pointed red nail. "You're such a mousey little thing."

"Obviously more than he saw in you," Cassie grated.

Isla's eyes glimmered like rubies as a sneer curled her full upper lip. They remained silent as they watched each other, Cassie warily, and Isla with a small gleam of satisfaction in her eyes. Cassie was unable to resist glancing back as she heard a dull thump. Dani had managed to drag Melissa's prone figure to the porch and was struggling to pull her up the stairs.

Isla took her brief distraction as an opportunity to pounce. Cassie caught the blur of motion out of the corner of her eye. Working on instinct, she spun around and swung out low with her foot. She connected with Isla's leg and knocked her slightly off balance, but it wasn't enough. Barely missing a beat, Isla grabbed hold of her leg, ripped her off her feet and threw her to the side.

A startled cry escaped her as she bounced across the ground. If it hadn't been for the mounds of snow she was certain she would have broken a few ribs, but the impact still knocked the breath out of her. She rolled to the side; dread filled her as she realized she'd lost the stake. It lay a few feet away from her, sticking straight up in the snow.

She quickly crawled toward it, but Isla was already coming at her again. Giving up on retrieving the stake, Cassie lurched to her feet and barely regained her balance before Isla slammed into her. Snow slid down Cassie's shirt and coated her skin as they fell back.

Grasping her turtleneck, Isla tightened it like a noose around her neck as she choked the air from her. Cassie fought against the hands clawing at her neck as she tried to block them from ripping her to shreds. Fisting her hand, she somehow managed to slam a solid blow against the side of Isla's face.

It only knocked Isla a little off balance, but it was enough so that Cassie was able to scramble backward. Isla recovered far quicker than Cassie had thought possible. She grabbed hold of Cassie's ankle and jerked her back toward her. A startled cry escaped Cassie; she kicked out, but her foot only glanced off of Isla's shoulder.

Isla pounced on her like a mountain lion. Bright stars burst before Cassie's eyes as adrenaline pounded through her in crashing waves. Isla sat on her chest, grinning like the cat that had just caught the canary. The last thing Cassie wanted to be was the canary.

Isla's eyes latched onto her neck and turned a volatile shade of red. Cassie realized that her turtleneck had been ripped down, and Devon's faded marks upon her were now clearly visible to Isla's acute vision. "Bitch," Isla sneered as her fangs cut into her bottom lip. "I'm going to drain you as dry as I drained your grandmother."

Cassie's breath was robbed from her as she went limp. Isla had killed her grandmother? *Isla?* Cassie had assumed it was Julian; with his ability, one brief touch would have allowed him access to Cassie's mind. It would have shown him who her grandmother was, where to look for her and what she looked like.

She'd never thought it was Isla, never realized it was *this* monster that had brutally ripped away the only blood relative Cassie had left and robbed the world of a cherished, loving soul.

Cassie's astonishment faded as rage blazed up to consume her in a cocoon of hatred and vengeance. It made the anger she'd experienced for the past two weeks look like a pitiful candle compared to the inferno kindling to life within her now. Her bones turned to cinder, and her muscles became ash as something else raced forward to consume her, to change her.

Something inside of her cracked. All reason fled as hatred and retribution roared to the forefront.

A flash of apprehension shimmered through Isla's eyes. Cassie had no idea what she saw that caused such a reaction, and she didn't care. Screaming with fury, Cassie found strength where there hadn't been any before. She would *destroy* this monster. No matter what, she was going to kill Isla, even if it meant going down with her. Gathering her legs beneath her, she heaved up with all her might, and with a strength she'd never possessed before. This power was unlike any she'd ever dreamed of, but it vitalized her as it pounded hotly through her veins. Isla's hold upon her was knocked loose as Cassie lifted her up and flipped her over top of her head.

Chest heaving, Cassie launched herself to her feet and spun hastily. Isla was just regaining her balance when Cassie raced forward. Isla tried to move away from her, but she wasn't quick enough as Cassie slammed into her and knocked them both into the snow.

～

DEVON PUSHED himself faster as he rounded the corner of the house. His mind honed in on Cassie's. He expected to feel terror or pain from her, but instead he found a depth of vehemence and hatred so entrenched and brutal it nearly knocked him back.

He skidded around the corner as Cassie flipped Isla over top of her head. Her shout echoed throughout the small backyard as Isla landed a few feet away. Cassie's golden hair whipped around her as she launched to her feet, her body was shaking not from the cold, but from something *far* worse.

An inner shudder went through him when he realized he wasn't too late to stop her death, but he may be too late to save her humanity.

"Cassie!" he bellowed. He raced forward as she bolted at Isla and knocked them both backward.

He bounded across the snow, forcing himself to move faster. He had to save her, he had to stop this. A flash of motion from the corner of his eye caused him to turn seconds before Julian crashed into him. Julian propelled them both against the side of the house with enough force to shake the wall.

"Not your battle!" Julian hissed in his ear. "Stay out of this Devon, you have to watch and learn. You must see what your little Hunter is capable of."

Devon was startled by the words, but he was able to shove Julian off of him. Devon lashed out and connected with a rapid uppercut that shot Julian's head back. His teeth clattered loudly together as he stumbled back. Julian's eyes gleamed as his grin revealed the length of his fangs. "Someone's been eating well," he murmured in amusement.

Devon snarled as he leapt forward. Julian dashed just out of Devon's grasp as he rapidly retreated toward the woods. "Don't forget about your girl," he taunted over his shoulder.

Devon spun back to the fight as Julian disappeared into the

woods, leaving Isla to fend for herself. "Coward!" Devon cried after him.

'You must to see what your little Hunter is capable of,' ran through his head. He was unnerved by what Julian might know, or suspect about her. There wasn't time to ponder it though as his mouth went dry at the spectacle before him.

CASSIE'S MIND had stopped thinking rational thought. All that mattered was destroying Isla and having the gratification of seeing her die. Though Isla was back on top of her, Cassie wasn't scared, but she could sense Isla's hesitance and confusion.

Isla struck at her, moving with the speed of a rattlesnake. Cassie merely grinned as her hand twisted around the stake she had managed to regain during their scuffle. Isla was only inches away from her when she drove the stake upward. Pleasure filled her at the satisfying crunch of bones as the stake pierced through her ribcage and drove deep into her heart. Isla's eyes widened as she pulled back and gazed down at Cassie in horror and disbelief. Cassie merely grinned back at her as she twisted the stake deeper. She didn't care that her joy was perverse and out of place here, she simply relished in the thrill filling her.

"Rot in Hell," she grated as Isla let out a low moan and collapsed on top of her.

Cassie just lay there for a moment, shaking with the emotions tearing through her. She thought she would find pleasure in destroying the woman who had murdered her grandmother, but there was none. Instead, there was only a hollow, lonely pit growing inside of her. A pit she was beginning to feel might never fill up and may just swallow her whole.

Taking ragged breaths she shoved Isla's corpse off of her. Though Isla was dead weight now, Cassie barely felt her burden against her trembling arms. She rolled to the side and dug her hands into the snow as she managed to lift herself onto her knees. Her muscles and bones shook as her whole body trembled and quaked. There was suddenly nothing inside of her but a budding sense of something else, of something wrong and very out of place. Something that didn't belong in her body at all, but it was growing inside of her and it was taking her by force as it consumed her.

Cassie moved one hand forward as she attempted to crawl away from the monster she'd just killed out of pure hatred. A hatred the likes of which she'd never experienced before, and hoped to never experience again. She couldn't shake the remnants of the hate, couldn't get away from whatever was inside of her.

Pain exploded through her. It constricted her muscles as it convulsed through them. Cassie wheezed as her fingers dug into the snow. A snow she could no longer feel the cold of because of the anguish tearing through her. It locked her extremities in place at the same time all her bones seemed to shatter and the fragments seemed to rip through her veins, muscles, and skin.

Wheezing for breath, a low, ragged groan escaped her. She heaved and shook, yet she remained completely locked in place in the snow. Snow flew up around her as Devon slid to a stop in front of her. "Cassie," he whispered, grasping hold of her shoulders.

His touch, normally so soothing, only sent fresh fire through her overly sensitized skin. Unable to stop it, a scream of pure torture ripped from her throat.

∾

PANIC PULSED through him as he took in her unyielding form. Her terror and disorientation radiated outward. "Cassie."

He gripped hold of her shoulders, knowing instantly he'd made the wrong choice. A scream ripped out of her and echoed eerily through the hushed night. She recoiled from him, but didn't get far as her body was completely rigid. He released her as a feeling of helplessness rolled through him.

"Cassie, Cassie, look at me."

Her head remained bowed as her body curled in on itself. He knew this feeling, vividly recalled the agony that had encompassed him and driven him to the brink of madness before blessed release finally took him under as he died. Except, she wasn't dying, not completely. No, what was happening to her was something *worse*.

"No," he moaned. He hated the vulnerability of this situation. He had to reach her and put a stop to this before he couldn't bring her back. "Cassie."

He barely grasped hold of her chin. Dread filled him as her eyes met his. The normally beautiful violet blue was gone. It had been replaced by a malevolent shade of red. His breath froze in his lungs; she didn't seem to see him as she unblinkingly stared forward.

"Cassie, you have to focus on me," he said as he searched out with his mind to try and grasp hold of hers. He had never *knowingly* exerted his power over her and he'd never meant to. Even when she'd left him, he'd never seriously considered taking control of her mind. But now... well now, he had no choice. She couldn't make the change completely, not without his blood, and he wasn't willing to do that to her.

He wouldn't condemn her to his life unless she made the choice willingly, and she wasn't doing that right now. Now it was being forced upon her by birth. *This* was not a choice she'd made, *this* was a cruel twist of fate, and he couldn't allow it to continue.

"Cassie," he murmured as he pushed through the fog clouding her mind. "Focus on me, look at *me*."

She shuddered again as a slight mewl escaped her. It took everything he had not to drag her against him to try and comfort her, but his touch would only distress her more. Frustration filled him, but he continued to probe against her mind as he tried to force his way in. She was awash in the sensations consuming her; reasonable thought was all but gone.

"What's going on? What's wrong with her?" Chris demanded.

Devon spun defensively as Chris and Melissa raced toward them. Their hair was still standing on end, and the smell of burnt hair and flesh radiated from them. Devon's lips pulled back, his teeth elongated. A snarl ripped from him as his protective urges sprang forth. If they came any closer they would hurt her, they would ruin everything. If they came any closer they would see her like this, something he knew she would hate.

"Stay back!" he commanded. They skidded to a halt a few feet away from him. Dani slid to a stop beside them and her mouth dropped. "Get away from her!"

They remained immobile as their eyes darted back and forth between the two of them. Cassie moaned again as a tremor wracked through her. Devon moved closer to shelter her from their eyes without touching her. Luther appeared suddenly, his face was a mask as his knowing eyes met Devon's gaze.

"Get inside," he ordered the others.

"Luther..."

"I said get inside!" he interrupted Melissa harshly. "There is nothing you can do here. You're only making it worse. Get inside!"

He pushed and shoved at them as he turned them forcefully away. "What is going on?" Chris demanded.

"I'll explain later. Go."

"The boy," Melissa reminded them.

Devon turned his full attention back to Cassie as Luther and Chris lifted the prone boy from the snow and hurried with him toward the house. Devon would have to take care of the child later, but for now his only concern was Cassie. She was still staring at him unseeingly, but she had wrapped her arms around her stomach and was curling into the fetal position.

"Listen to me Cassie, you can beat this. You are strong enough to beat this. You can do this Cassie. I know you can," he urged.

He slipped past the barrier as he took complete control of her mind. He whispered soothing words to her, as he sought the spirit he knew still had to reside within her. It took longer than he would have liked, but eventually he found it.

Seizing hold of it, he wrapped his presence around hers as he attempted to shelter her from the changes trying to take her over. He felt her coming back as his strength helped her to fight against the centuries of blood and heritage that had pushed her to this brink of insanity.

"You can do this," he whispered aloud.

Finally her muscles began to ease. She blinked as her eyes flickered between the explosive red and the dazzling violet blue he loved so dearly. Blinking again, her eyes locked onto his as tears spilled down her reddened cheeks. "Devon," she whispered.

He caught her as she collapsed into the snow and unconsciousness dragged her under.

CHAPTER TEN

DEVON KEPT CASSIE on his lap and the blanket wrapped snuggly around her. Though she had showered, she was still chilled, and her skin was abnormally pale. It was not the lingering effects of the snow that held her within its grasp though, but the remnants of pain. He pulled her more firmly against him as he cradled her. She rested her head in the hollow of his neck as a small shiver worked its way through her.

Kissing the top of her head, he rubbed her arms as he attempted to return some heat to her body. She wiggled against him as she tried to get closer. He didn't think that would last once she heard what he and Luther had to say. He glanced up at Luther, uncertain where to start, or if they should start at all. They had all been traumatized tonight. Chris and Melissa continued to jerk involuntarily once in a while from the lasting effects of Isla's electrical current. Dani looked like she had seen a ghost as she glanced rapidly between him and Cassie and then around the room.

Luther was still distraught over the boy, who thankfully

hadn't sustained enough blood loss to warrant a hospital, but whose parents had been frantic when they'd been called. Isla's body had been hidden until the sun found it in the morning, and turned it to cinder. Devon was surprised to find himself still beyond the level of strength he was used to feeling, especially after exerting his will over Cassie and the boy. Cassie's blood in his veins had kept him stronger than he would have been at any other point in time.

Chris's right hand jerked on the armrest of the loveseat. He scowled down at the offending extremity as he slapped hold of it with his other hand. "How long are the effects going to last?" he muttered miserably.

"Probably till tomorrow," Luther answered absently.

Chris's scowl deepened as he gave Luther a disgruntled look. "Wonderful."

Melissa fisted her hands as she tried to keep herself still. She was fighting a losing battle. "Are you going to tell us what happened out there?" she demanded.

Luther glanced at him and Devon gave a brief nod. Luther knew more about what was going on than he did. Luther paced over to the fireplace mantel and rested his arm on top of it. "A few weeks ago Devon came to me with some doubts and concerns." Cassie's forehead furrowed questioningly as she glanced up at him. "I agreed there were some things we should look into where you're concerned."

"What kind of doubts and questions?" Cassie inquired.

Devon hated to do this to her, but it had to be done. "I had some questions about you."

Her delicate hands fisted in her lap. "I don't understand," she whispered.

"Devon had some questions about the Hunter line, specifically questions about Hunters with your abilities," Luther qualified.

"I don't have any abilities."

"I have told you many times your enhanced speed, hearing, sight, and strength are all abilities."

"Ok fine," Cassie relented. "But why would there be any questions about that?"

"Because," Devon said. "Your abilities are so very close to mine, and to other vampires."

Cassie jolted but her face was still marred with confusion. Chris and Melissa looked just as baffled; Dani still radiated a peculiar alarm. "All of us have enhanced speed, hearing, and sight, so what are you saying?" Chris demanded, not at all in the mood to be patient.

"The day Cassie's grandmother died, Cassie was so angry at me when she turned on me her eyes flashed red," Devon said as Cassie became rigid against him. "That was when I went to Luther."

"Why didn't you tell me?" she whispered.

"You weren't exactly talking to me at the time." Her fingers picked at the blanket.

"We decided to do some research," Luther continued. "We began to look for information about the Hunters who had been like Cassie, but there was little to find as there hasn't been one in the past three hundred years. I had to turn to some of my Guardian friends for help. One of them possessed a book that was of great interest to me, and helped to answer some questions, but also raised more."

Luther frowned thoughtfully as he thought over his next words. "Please stop speaking in riddles and just tell us what is going on," Cassie demanded.

Luther met her gaze as he nodded. "The last Hunter like you, that was actually recorded, was three hundred years ago. Her name was Gertrude, and during a large battle Gertrude became so infuriated and blood thirsty she began to change into a vampire."

Cassie's mouth dropped as her gaze flitted between Devon and Luther. Devon remained perfectly still, terrified she would turn against him as soon as this was all over. "Wait, wait." Chris held up a hand. "Are you saying this woman actually became a *vampire*?"

Luther tugged at his hair. "No, she didn't have enough vampire blood in her to make the change successfully. She was caught in between."

Cassie's hands clasped the blanket in her lap. "She became one of those *things*, those monsters that get stuck in between?" she croaked out.

"Yes," Devon answered.

"Are you saying I could do the same?"

"Yes." Devon winced at the horrified look filling her eyes. Chris and Melissa gasped; Dani became as still as stone. "That's what happened to you outside, and it's also how you were able to defeat Isla. Your powers increased when your fury became so intense that it allowed your vampire DNA to take hold of you."

The room became so still he could hear the subtle crackling of the power lines outside. Cassie was as unmoving as a cement block as she absorbed everything. "This woman, Gertrude, what happened to her?" she inquired in a strangled voice.

"Unfortunately, she had to be destroyed. She couldn't be allowed to survive," Luther told her.

Chris's breath exploded from him as he leapt to his feet. He ran his hand through his hair, tugging at the singed shaggy blond strands as he cursed viciously. "Are you kidding me?" Melissa demanded. "That's bull! I don't understand why that would happen; we were all created the same way!"

Luther pulled his glasses off to clean them. "I'm not one hundred percent certain, but I believe that when a Hunter has an ability the vampire blood in them is more dispersed in order to help fuel the gift the Hunter possesses. When a Hunter doesn't have a gift, the vampire blood in them is more concentrated. They are stronger and faster, with better senses. More like a vampire themselves."

They continued to gawk at Luther while Cassie remained unmoving. Devon heard the increased beat of her heart and felt the chill that washed over her skin. Her eyes were tumultuous and lost as she turned back to him. He yearned to do something to ease the torment radiating from her, but there was nothing. All he could do was be here for her, and try to comfort her.

"I... I don't understand, what does all this mean? Am I a danger? Am I going to turn into one of these things at a moment's notice? Or will it take something more, like Isla telling me she killed my grandmother?"

Devon's hands constricted on her. "*Isla* killed your grandmother?"

"Yes, she told me that tonight. That was when..." she broke off as her voice failed her for a minute. "That was when I lost control, when the rage took over. It was awful."

He rubbed her back as he tried to comfort her. He'd never considered that Isla had been the one who killed her grandmother; they had all just assumed it was Julian. Anger boiled through him, but he kept it hidden from her.

"But I don't understand," Cassie mused. "Wouldn't I still be weaker than a vampire? I mean I'm not fully one of them, so wouldn't they still be able to beat me? Shouldn't Isla have still won?"

This was the one thing Devon had hoped she wouldn't question. He met Luther's gaze, but he knew Luther wouldn't be the one to explain this. "No Cassie," Devon told her. "You would think so, but the things that get stuck in the middle, they're mindless. A vampire may be more powerful, but they still have a survival instinct, these things..." He trailed off simply because this was the part he didn't like to think about. "These things don't. All they crave is the kill; all they experience is the blood-lust. They care nothing for their own lives, all they aim to do is destroy and massacre."

Cassie's eyes swirled with confusion as she stared at him. Then the color drained out of her face. He thought she was going to fall over. He tightened his hold on her as he tried to keep her from withdrawing from him again.

"Cassie..."

"I'm a monster," she breathed.

"No..."

She jerked away from him and launched to her feet with startling grace and speed. He tried to reach for her again, but she had already moved beyond his grasp as she paced to the doorway. Her hands were shaking; her skin was so white now he could see the small blue veins running through her porcelain complexion. Her lips had turned nearly as white as the rest of her.

"I really *am* a monster," she whispered.

"Cassie no..."

Chris broke off as she turned on him. "I'm not even like you guys," she said flatly. "I'm nothing. I'm a walking threat to this planet..."

"That is not true!" Luther cut in brusquely. "There were other Hunters like you before Gertrude who never had any problems. Gertrude was a one in a million occurrence, the rest were fine."

Devon rose as Cassie turned away from them. Though it looked as if she were about to leave, she remained where she was. "But it's already happened to me. It *will* happen again."

"You don't know that!" Chris protested.

Though she still looked shell shocked, a cold acceptance had settled around her. Devon felt his stomach drop as he realized the Cassie he'd wanted back was gone. That Cassie, though she'd had a difficult life and had lost a lot, had still maintained some of her innocence. This Cassie was still the same, and yet she was so very different. She was more resilient and more knowing. This Cassie wouldn't turn against him and she wouldn't try to block out the world by hiding behind a wall. This Cassie would face it head on and beat it down with her bare fists if she had to.

He'd sought to keep her sheltered from this harsh reality of her life, but he knew now it had been inevitable. She knew far more of the cruelty of the world than most people, but it wouldn't destroy her. Like a phoenix rising from the ashes, he watched as she became more mature, more solid, an adult, a woman.

"I do know that Chris," she said forcefully. "I know what is inside of me now; I know what is just beneath the surface. I *felt* that hatred and frenzy and it is something you can never understand, and I don't want you to." There was a sad acceptance in her eyes as she turned to him. For the first time she truly understood him and what it was he went through daily. "And now that it has been released I will have to constantly struggle to keep it suppressed. I *know* that."

It wasn't a struggle he'd wished for her to go through, but there was nothing he could do to change it. He could only stand by her, and do what he could to make sure she didn't step over that precipice for good.

"It's ok though," she continued as she turned her attention back to Chris, and a small smile tugged at the corner of her mouth.

"Cassie," Melissa said softly, unable to keep the heartache from her voice.

"No, it really is ok. It makes things easier."

"Excuse me?" Luther inquired.

Her eyes found Devon's again. "It makes the choice so much easier, it really does."

Devon froze as hope nearly drowned him in its suffocating, pounding waves. "Do you mean?" he barely managed to squeeze the words out through the sudden constriction in his chest. He had dreamed of this moment, and now that it was finally here, he didn't want to hear the words. Because they were words he was afraid he couldn't fulfill.

Her smile grew, and although she was still unnaturally pale, there was a glow about her. "Yes," she breathed. "I can't get stuck in between if I'm already all the way over. I'll join you, Devon."

CHAPTER ELEVEN

C<small>ASSIE</small> <small>HEARD</small> the collective inhalation of breaths, but she couldn't tear her gaze away from Devon. The longing radiating from him warmed her heart, caused her toes to curl, and made every scary thing about her decision completely right. It would be ok; he could calm the raging insanity in her. He could help her control it and he could make it so she wouldn't be some creature stuck in the middle, lost to a world of lunacy and blood-lust. He could do all of that for her, and for the first time, she had no fear about letting him do so.

This was right, this was what she wanted, and it would be good. She knew that. Between them, things would be good, forever.

Even if she hadn't just learned she could lose complete control of herself, and everything she believed in, she knew she'd made the right choice. She would have made it anyway; this new knowledge had just precipitated it faster. No matter what, she would have chosen to spend forever with him.

"Cassie," Chris said. "Are you sure?"

She turned away from Devon and braced herself for the aversion she was sure would be on their faces. She loved them all dearly, but she had made her choice and she was going to stick by it. She was surprised there was no disgust there, however. Chris and Melissa looked as if they'd been expecting this; Dani had retreated to the window and wasn't looking at them. It was only Luther who didn't look happy.

"Yes."

"I'm sorry, but you can't."

Cassie's head shot toward Luther as irritation and frustration rolled through her. She hadn't expected her decision to be met with open arms, but she had expected some of Luther's prejudice's against Devon to have lessened. They had worked together in order to find out more about the Hunters like her after all.

"Luther..."

He held up a hand to stall her irritated tirade. His gaze was sad and lost. Cassie's mouth snapped shut in the face of his distress. He glanced toward Devon, opened his mouth and then closed it again. Taking a deep breath, Luther rubbed the bridge of his nose before meeting her gaze once more. "Cassie, we don't know what will happen to you if you are changed."

She frowned fiercely at him before turning to Devon. His eyes were dark and treacherous as they glimmered in the light. It was the despair in his gaze that caused her heart to turn over, and her stomach to plummet.

"No Hunter has ever been changed," Luther continued. "There is no way of knowing what it might bring. You already have vampire DNA in you, more so than most Hunters. We don't know what would happen to any Hunter who is changed; let alone what will happen to *you*. You are so close to the precipice now."

Cassie fought to keep breathing through the anxiety clutching at her. "Devon can help with that," she managed to say.

"Devon was able to bring you back before, but if he changes you and you become something more, he may not be able to pull you back. Ever."

There was a downtrodden slope to his shoulders that only confirmed Luther's words. "Devon?" she whispered.

"There is already a demon in you Cassie," he said reluctantly. "Luther is right. There is no way to know."

The breath wheezed out of her as hope deflated from her like a popped balloon. "So, that's it then," she said. "There's nothing we can do."

"I'm not saying that, Cass," Luther said kindly. "I'm just saying we have to take our time, do some more research. I've never heard of a Hunter being turned, but it may have happened, and there may be something out there that would tell us about it. I'd never thought to look for anything about *you*, until Devon came to me, and now we will look for information about *this*."

"No," Devon said forcefully. "No more digging, no more research." Cassie felt as if her legs were going to give out, but she somehow managed to keep herself standing upright. Didn't he want to figure this all out somehow and end both of their misery? "It's too risky."

Cassie blinked at him, Melissa and Chris looked just as confused as she was. "Risky?" she inquired.

Devon nodded briskly. "The Commission, if they know you exist they will come for you. They will destroy you Cassie."

"No, they won't!" she and Chris protested simultaneously.

Melissa's mouth parted as she took an abrupt step forward. Dani finally turned away from the window to survey them. "That's why no other Hunters like Cassie were recorded, not after Gertrude anyway," Melissa whispered, antipathy and understanding evident in her voice. "The *Commission* destroyed them."

Bile rose up Cassie's throat. "Why?" she breathed. "Why would they do that?"

Luther took a deep breath, but it was Devon who answered her. "Because they cannot, and *will* not, allow a fault in the bloodlines. They couldn't take the chance that one of their creations might turn against them, and become more destructive than the monsters they had been created to destroy."

Cassie gaped at him as Chris cursed loudly; he turned on his heel and restlessly paced the room as he tugged at his hair. Melissa slumped against the wall, and Cassie was surprised by the single tear sliding down her face. Dani stared at them with large eyes, and her mouth parted as she rapidly glanced around the room.

"I know you don't like the idea, but I think it's a very good idea you leave this town now. Luther tried to be discreet, but if they put two and two together, they will come for you."

Cassie's eyes shot back to Devon as her jaw dropped. "You can't be serious! They wouldn't do such a thing!"

"Yes, Cassie, I believe they would," Luther confirmed.

Her legs felt like Jell-O as she slid to the floor. Hadn't she already given up enough? What more could life take from her? What more could it throw at her? Now she had to worry about her own kind coming after her, and there was a distinct possibility she couldn't join Devon without becoming a complete monstrosity.

Devon was instantly in front of her, his solid strength seeped into her as he took hold of her hands. "We *will* get through this," he said forcefully as his spectacular emerald eyes blazed into hers. "We will get through this, we will get it all sorted out, and we *will* be together Cassie. No matter what it takes, we will be together. But first we must think about your safety, *all* of you have to go somewhere safe."

Cassie tried to be reassured by his words, tried to believe in them, but she couldn't quench all of her doubts. She swallowed heavily and nodded firmly. She had to believe him; otherwise she wouldn't be able to keep on going, to keep on fighting. There had to be a light at the end of this dark tunnel, or she was going to succumb to the darkness inside her. She knew she would.

"You're right, we will be," she agreed as she managed a wan smile for him. His hands constricted around hers, a small twinkle lit his eyes. He helped lift her to her feet and wrapped his arm around her waist as he pulled her close to him. "But why would they come for all of us, I thought it was only me they wanted?"

"It may be more than The Commission that comes here now, Cassie."

"Excuse me?" Chris demanded.

Cassie's hand tensed in Devon's shirt. "What do you mean?" she inquired.

"Isla is dead Cassie; you are *the* Hunter, and *only* one who killed her. That is a feat that would have been thought impossible, before today. Isla was a Grounder, she was nearly an Elder, and far stronger than *any* other vampire you have defeated. When word of that spreads, others will come to take their chance at you. Julian will not fight alone, he knows he can't win, but he won't leave either. You are far too much of a challenge for him to quit now. They will come for you, Cass, but they will go after all of you now that they know you are here."

Chris exploded in a flurry of curses. Cassie merely gawked at Devon as weird sputtering noises escaped her; she could barely catch her breath. A loud crash snapped her head around. Chris was staring bashfully at them as he held his dust covered hand up. Behind him there was a hole in the wall. "Sorry," he mumbled.

"That solved things," Melissa muttered as she shook her head. "I'll get you some ice."

"Are you ok?" Dani inquired as Melissa hurried from the room.

Chris nodded, but heat colored his face as he kept his gaze diverted. Melissa returned to the room with ice wrapped in a towel. "Next time don't blame it on the wall."

He gave her a small smile as he took the towel from her. "So what do we do now?" Melissa inquired as she returned to her place by the mantle.

"I've made some phone calls; I have a safe place for the five of you to go."

"What about you?" Cassie demanded.

He shook his head. "Someone has to stay. They will come for you, but they will only stay until they discover you're gone. They may cause some damage during that time though, so someone must be here to stop them."

"Absolutely not!" Cassie declared forcefully. "I will not leave you here alone to fight against them. You may be strong Devon, but you are not that strong!"

"Cassie..."

"No! No, I cannot lose you too, it would destroy me!" The very thought of it made her long to curl into a ball at the same time she had the urge to destroy everything. It was a feeling she realized was extremely hazardous to her, to all of them now. "We are not leaving Devon."

"It will only be for a little bit, and it is best you aren't here right now. Not until you can get a better grip on what is going on inside of you."

"And what if it takes over when you're not there?" she demanded, determined not to be forced from this town. They were needed here to protect people, and she couldn't be separated from him. "I can't come back from it if you're not there! And what if you're killed?"

"Easy Cassie." His voice took on a soothing tone that set her teeth on edge.

"I'm not a child!" she retorted. "Don't talk to me like I am."

His eyes became darker as he studied her. "I know, but you have got to keep your emotions under control."

She scowled up at him as she tried to keep her annoyance and terror in check. "You can't stay here alone."

He nodded as he pulled her close and dropped a kiss on her forehead. "I have figured something out."

"Devon..."

"Cassie, the safety of each one of you is of the utmost importance."

"Where would we go?" Chris demanded.

Devon's hand wrapped around the back of her head as he slid his fingers smoothly through her hair and held her close. "You would agree to leave?" he asked.

Chris stared at Cassie for a moment before nodding slowly. "If The Commission and *more* vampires come for Cassie, we can't stop them all. We won't be enough. The last thing I would like to do is leave, the people here..." he shook his head as his gaze flitted to the window. "We can't leave them unprotected. My mother."

"I'll make sure they're safe."

"And what about *your* safety?" Cassie was unwilling to concede yet and leave him here while they were exiled.

"I'll have help," he murmured.

"Who?" Melissa inquired. "If we go, *who* will you have to help you?"

A sinking sensation settled in her stomach as Devon's eyes pleaded with her for understanding. "I called Annabelle and Liam." Cassie's mouth dropped as her breath exploded from her. "They're on their way."

"What?" she gasped.

"Who are Annabelle and Liam?" Melissa's delicate brow was furrowed in confusion as she glanced between the two of them.

"Annabelle is a vampire I created," Devon explained, but his eyes remained locked on Cassie's.

She could see the plea in his gaze to be ok with this, to understand. She couldn't find the words to reassure him though, she didn't know how to. She didn't know how she felt about this. He had once thought himself in love with Annabelle, *she* was the reason he didn't feed on humans anymore. Cassie knew he was completely in love with her, and had never truly loved Annabelle, she still couldn't help but feel unsettled and confused.

"Liam will stay here with me, and you will go with Annabelle."

Cassie's heart turned over as panic filled her. "Devon..."

"It's for the best Cassie. They have a place further up north where you can all stay until this has blown over and we can figure out something better."

"And if I lose control again?" she whispered.

"Annabelle is a healer; she may be able to pull you back."

"It's a good possibility," Luther agreed.

Cassie wanted to protest, she wanted to cry. She wanted to absolutely refuse to leave his side. But she couldn't find the words, and she knew they would only fall upon deaf ears. "When are they coming?" Melissa inquired.

"They were leaving Pennsylvania at sunset; hopefully they'll be here by morning."

"My grandmother's home, her things..."

"I'll make sure everything is taken care of Cassie, I promise. Nothing bad will happen to your home."

Cassie turned away from him as she took in the living room. This was the only home she'd ever known, all of her things were here. All of her *grandmother's* things were here. She blinked back the tears burning her eyes as she strained to keep them from spilling over. She would come back here, one day, she *would* come back.

"And if my mother decides to stay behind?" Chris asked.

"I will watch over her too," Devon assured him.

Cassie instantly began to protest. "But this town, these people..."

"Will be safe. I am an Elder and Liam is a powerful vampire in his own right. If The Commission comes, they won't be a threat, and neither will the vampires once they realize only Liam and I are here."

Cassie swallowed heavily as she fought the urge to scream in frustration. "And what if The Elders decide to come looking for us?" Melissa asked.

Cassie's stomach dropped at the thought. Devon's arm constricted around her as he shook his head. "The Elders have been in hiding for almost fifteen years, and before that they'd retreated for nearly a hundred years. They won't come out now, not even for this. They hate the world, they have for centuries. They may have orchestrated and participated in The Slaughter but that was to wipe out The Hunter line..."

"And now that they know it isn't wiped out?" Cassie interrupted.

Devon shook his head. "It's decimated enough not to overly concern them. They figure the rest of the vampires, with any sense, will be able to take out the remaining stragglers. That is why I must keep you safe now."

Cassie looked helplessly toward Chris, Melissa, and Dani as she tried to come up with some other argument, some brilliant plan none of them had thought of yet. But they looked just as dumbfounded as she felt.

"I suppose we should pack then," Melissa said.

CHAPTER TWELVE

CASSIE WAS STANDING by the window when he entered her room. Her hair cascaded around her and the glow of the moon caused it to shimmer a silvery gold. Her arms were wrapped around her stomach as she stared out at the dark night. She turned toward him; her eyes haunted and lost as she watched him.

"You will come back to me," she whispered.

Swallowing heavily, he managed a small, reassuring nod. "I will *always* come back to you."

She nodded as her arms fell back to her sides. "Really?"

He hated the doubt and apprehension he sensed in her. "Of course."

There was a defeated slouch to her shoulders as she turned back to the window. "You told me once I would have to join you, or you would have to leave me. You told me you didn't think you could continue to control yourself around me, and now it seems as if I will never be able to join you."

"We don't know that for sure," he reminded her.

"No, but it is a good possibility. Will you be able to stay around me?"

She looked up in startled surprise as he crossed the room to her. "I was a fool to say that to you Cassie. I was wrong, and I was being selfish. I *can* stay with you. I *will* stay with you, no matter what it takes. No matter what I have to do, I will not leave you."

"I felt your need; I felt your struggle Devon. You fed from me; you were a part of me, inside of me. I know how challenging it is for you to be around me, and I don't want you to have to go through that all the time."

He seized hold of her hands and pulled her forward a step. Clasping hold of her face, he pushed her hair aside to stroke her silken cheek. "Cassie I would go through Hell and back if it meant being by your side. We *will* get through this, I swear to you we will."

She bit her bottom lip as her gaze fell away. "But the fight you have to wage with yourself is..."

"Is easier now," he interrupted. "It is much easier now Cassie. Letting me feed on you helped to ease the hunger."

Her eyes flew back up to his as she searched his face. He tried to keep his expression as impassive as he could. Though it wasn't entirely the truth, it wasn't a lie either. When she'd given her blood, she'd helped to ease the demon inside him. However, it wouldn't be entirely appeased until she was by his side, safely immortal, but he wasn't about to tell her that. Not when there was a chance he would never be able to turn her.

He shoved the thought aside, unable to deal with it right now. The monster inside him didn't like that knowledge. Neither did the man. He couldn't stand the thought of her growing old and dying while he stayed young and alive. He wished the sun's rays were still deadly to him, because the minute he lost her, he would walk straight into them.

"Devon..."

"It will be ok Cassie, everything will be ok," he promised. "Once the threat passes, we'll see if we can't find some more information, without drawing attention to ourselves again, ok?"

He could see the doubt in her gaze, but she managed a small nod. "Ok. You had better keep yourself safe."

"I will," he promised as he bent to kiss the tip of her nose.

Holding his face in her hands she dropped a tender kiss on his lips. "Will you feed from me tonight?" she murmured.

Excitement spurted through him as his hands clenched upon her. His jaw locked as he glanced out the window. He had almost lost her tonight, and there was still the very awful possibility he would lose her. There were so many people, and things out there trying to tear them apart or kill them. The thought was so tempting but he knew he shouldn't. "I don't think that's a good idea Cassie, it's too soon..."

"I feel fine, I swear, and we don't know how long we're going to be apart," her voice broke. "It will be all right Devon, but I need this tonight, and I think you do too."

Then, she leaned up and kissed him again. The subtle brush of her lips against his robbed him of all reason. He pulled her closer, and she melded to him, pressing flush to him as her legs gave out. He swung her easily into his arms as she burrowed closer to him. He refused to acknowledge this might be their last night together for a while. If he dwelled on it too much he was scared he may break and change her. It was the worst thing he could do right now. He didn't know what she would become if she was changed, or if he could stop her if she became something truly malevolent.

The thought terrified him. For all her faults, Cassie was still everything good and loving, for that to be taken away from her was something he couldn't allow to happen. No matter how badly he desired her with him, he had to come to terms with the possibility it could never happen. He just didn't intend to realize that tonight.

Tonight was simply about the two of them, and that was the way he was going to keep it.

He laid her down on the bed and followed behind as he pulled her against him once more. He lost himself in the touch and feel and scent of her as he shut out the rest of the world, and the far too many people trying to tear them apart.

~

CASSIE COULDN'T STOP NERVOUSLY RINGING her hands as she paced before her window. She glanced back at Devon, who was still sleeping with his arm tossed over the spot she'd recently vacated. Though she'd only gotten a couple hours of sleep, she was wide awake. The sun would be up soon, Annabelle and Liam might also be here soon.

She didn't know how she felt about that. Though she didn't like the idea of leaving here, she wanted to get this over and done with. The sooner it was over, the sooner she could be with Devon again. Her skin crawled; her chest constricted at the thought of being apart from him for any significant length of time. If it hadn't been for the irrational anger fueling her, she never would have made it through the two weeks without him. How would she get through it now, when she wasn't enraged?

In fact, she was terrified. Terrified of losing him, of what she was now, and what she could become. What if something happened and he wasn't there to pull her back, and Annabelle was also unable to? She would be lost forever, a monster, a threat to everyone she loved. Cassie shuddered as she stared down at the deserted street.

Then there was Annabelle herself. She didn't know how to feel about meeting the woman who had so drastically changed Devon. The woman who had made him the man he was now. Though he had never truly loved her, Annabelle had been a huge impact on his life, and she was very special to him.

Cassie tried not to feel jealous, but she couldn't help it. Leaning forward, she rested her fingers against the window, enjoying the cool feel of it. Arms wrapped around her waist and caused a small cry of surprise to escape her. He had been completely noiseless in his approach. Devon hugged her close as he pressed her back firmly against his chest. His lips brushed over the fresh marks on her neck. Cassie shivered in response, her skin tingled all over as a feeling of rightness stole through her.

"Are you ok?" he inquired.

"Yes."

He ran his hands over her stomach as he kissed her once more. "Couldn't sleep?"

She shook her head as she savored his strength and comfort. She could stay like this forever, but they had such a short amount of time. "No."

Beams splayed across the road, illuminating the street as a vehicle turned onto it. Cassie stiffened as the silver Cadillac Escalade pulled to a stop in front of the house and doused the lights. "They're here," Devon murmured.

Cassie managed a small nod. "Yes."

"Come on." Devon pulled reluctantly away and took hold of her hand. Cassie followed behind; she fought to maintain her outward composure, while inside she was falling apart. Her hand squeezed around his to the point where she knew it had to be uncomfortable for him, but he didn't protest, or try to pull away. They were at the top of the steps as the doorbell sounded.

Chris appeared in the hallway, his hair was disheveled from sleep, his eyes bleary as he blinked up at them. Dani poked her head out from her room. Though her short, pink streaked hair was standing straight up, she didn't appear to have been asleep as she studied them with questioning eyes. "Your friends?" she asked.

"Yes," Devon answered as he started down the stairs.

Cassie was tempted to jerk him back and stop him, but she couldn't. Though she would have loved a few more minutes to get her thoughts together, and her rolling emotions under control, she knew she couldn't leave them standing on her doorstep. They were here to help after all.

Chris watched her with a sad gleam in his sapphire eyes. She scowled at him, disliking that he could sense the nervousness, jealousy, and uncertainty tearing through her. He managed a small nod and a listless smile for her as Devon strode past with his hand still wrapped around hers. She could only stare help-lessly back at Chris while Devon threw the locks and pulled open the door.

Taking a deep breath, Cassie turned her attention to the two people on her porch. Her heart plummeted as it flipped over and a thrumming tension pulsed through her. "Devon!" the young woman, Annabelle, cried. Stepping forward, she moved to embrace him, only to halt abruptly. She grinned at him as she cocked a strawberry colored eyebrow in amusement. Her thick, strawberry blond hair tumbled in loose curls to just below her shoulder blades.

"Cassie." Cassie jumped as Devon turned to her, his emerald eyes gleamed with amusement. "You have to invite them in."

"Oh," she replied stupidly. "Of course, umm, come on in."

She took a step back, releasing Devon's hand as Annabelle moved through the door and embraced him. Cassie looked quickly away, her stomach twisting as she tried to keep her jealousy and uneasiness under control. Understanding and strength radiated from Chris as he met her gaze.

"You must be Cassie." Annabelle was suddenly before her. Cassie jolted as the girl clasped hold of her hands and enfolded them in hers. Her sea green eyes were vivid, a wealth of compassion and care radiated in them. Her features were delicate, perfect, and a hint of freckles spattered her tiny nose. "It's a pleasure to meet you."

Cassie stared down at the woman, who was a good five inches shorter than her. She couldn't help but return Annabelle's radiant smile. She emitted warmth and friendship more than any person Cassie had ever met, and she couldn't help but instantly like her. "You also," she said softly.

Annabelle's smile grew; her eyes twinkled as she squeezed Cassie's hands once more before letting go. The tall, slender man who had come with Annabelle stepped forward to take hold of Cassie's hand. His dark brown hair fell in waves around his handsome, open face. His startling, oddly silver colored eyes burned into her as he studied her carefully.

"It's nice to meet you," he said in a lilting voice that held the hint of a Midwest accent.

"You too," she whispered, surprised by the man with the strange silver eyes. He seemed pleasant enough, but there was a shy reservation in him that didn't seem to fit in with the open warmth Annabelle radiated.

"And this is Chris." Devon drew their attention away from Cassie. Chris shook hands with them as he exchanged quick, pleasant greetings.

"Where are the others?" Annabelle inquired.

"Dani should be coming down soon," Cassie answered, surprised to realize she hadn't followed them downstairs. "Luther and Melissa went home to pack, but they'll be back before daybreak. Though I suppose we can't go anywhere till night anyway."

"Of course we can," Annabelle replied airily. "The windows are fully tinted so if I stay in the back I'll be fine. Besides, Julian won't be able to watch us if we depart during the daylight hours."

Cassie felt dread set in again as she glanced at Chris, who looked just as surprised as she felt. It was too soon to leave; she'd been expecting another full day in her home. Devon stepped closer to her and encircled her waist as he pulled her against him and pressed his lips against her ear.

"It will be ok," he promised.

Cassie managed a small nod, but she couldn't shake the knot of tension wrapping through her chest. Annabelle was watching them closely, amusement evident in her eyes. "I think the sooner the better," she told him.

Devon's arms tightened around Cassie before he nodded briskly. "You're right."

Closing her eyes, she buried her head against his chest as she labored to keep on breathing. "Hello."

Cassie lifted her head as Dani appeared at the bottom of the stairs. Her gold streaked eyes were narrowed as she surveyed Annabelle and Liam. "Hello!" Annabelle greeted as she glided over to the tiny girl. Even with as petite as Dani was, Annabelle was smaller. Annabelle seized hold of Dani's hands as she flashed her radiant smile. "And who are you?"

Dani managed a feeble smile. "Danielle," she answered. "But you can call me Dani."

"It's a pleasure to meet you Dani. This is my mate, Liam."

"Mate?" Cassie couldn't help but inquire.

Annabelle flashed a grin back at Cassie. Liam moved behind Annabelle and rested his hands upon her delicate shoulders. "Yes, my mate. You haven't explained this to her yet Devon?"

Cassie was surprised by the severity of Devon's eyes as he stared at Annabelle. "No," he grated.

Annabelle's frown intensified; her eyes became dark and turbulent as she glanced between the two of them. What was it he hadn't told her? What could he possibly be keeping from her? "I see," she whispered.

"What is a mate?" Chris inquired.

"It is what a vampire takes, or the bond they create, when they find the person or vampire, they choose to spend eternity with. It is a very profound experience." Annabelle's forehead was furrowed as she met Devon's gaze again. "And it's binding."

"So, it's like, vampire marriage?" Chris asked in surprise. "Cause that sounds a little strange."

"And why is that?" Liam inquired in a low, gravelly tone.

Chris shrugged as he ran his hand through his hair and tugged at it. "I don't know. I mean you're dead and all, and you do live forever. Seems a little strange you would choose to be with the same person that whole time; I can barely contemplate thirty years with the same person, never mind an eternity with them."

"Chris!" Cassie scolded as she shook her head at him. What Annabelle was describing seemed like an intense, private experience. It didn't sound like something that should be talked about so flippantly, or mocked, and it sounded like something she desperately wanted to experience with Devon.

"What?" he inquired defensively. "It's true!"

Annabelle merely grinned at him while Liam shook his head. "When you find the *one* person you can't spend the rest of your life without you will understand, and believe me thirty years will seem like a second," Annabelle replied. "And the taking of a mate is not something that is entered into lightly. As I said it is binding, and unbreakable. You are tied to a mate forever."

"So both mates have to be vampires?" Chris inquired as he stared at Cassie, and then Devon.

"Yes," Annabelle continued. "The bond is created through the sharing of blood and sex."

Cassie felt as if someone had kicked her in the gut as the air rushed out of her. Everyone else remained silent as Annabelle's words sank in. Cassie turned toward Devon and tilted her head to look up at him. He had taken her blood, but she was acutely aware he hadn't shared his, and neither had they forged a bond through sex. It wasn't that she was afraid to anymore, or that she still had doubts she wouldn't be enough for him, because she knew she would. She just wanted it to happen when there was no one out there trying to kill them.

Although, she realized that may be the impossible dream. It was likely there would never be a time when someone wasn't trying to kill them, and she didn't want to die without having shared the experience with him. But the sharing of blood was something they may never be able to experience. She was surprised by how disappointed she was by the realization. She thought she should be repulsed by it, but she wasn't. Not if it was Devon's blood.

Why hadn't he told her about this? Had he kept it from her because he didn't feel she was his mate? Didn't he feel the same way about her, as she did about him? A cold chill curdled in her belly; her skin turned to ice as everything in her went numb. But that couldn't be true, she'd felt his emotions, she *knew* how intensely he felt about her.

He seemed to sense her distress as he pulled her closer against him. Annabelle's eyes were questioning as she studied them and Cassie didn't like the scrutiny she found herself under. "I'll get my things," Dani interrupted before she turned and hurried up the stairs.

"I uh... I should go get my things too, and say goodbye to my mom," Chris said.

"She's not coming with us?" Cassie blurted out, forgetting all about her fright and confusion in the face of Chris's statement.

He shook his head sadly. "No, she doesn't want to leave, and I suppose there is no reason for her to. She's not one of *us* after all."

Cassie felt the sorrow behind his words. He may not have been close with his mother, but he still loved her, and he always would. When they left here though, there was a good possibility he may never see her again. "Would you like me to come with you?" Cassie asked.

He hesitated before shaking his head. "No, I'd better do this alone."

Cassie nodded reluctantly. Chris moved past Liam and threw the door open to the sun breaking on the horizon. "I'll put your car in the garage." Devon stepped forward to claim the keys from Liam.

Cassie watched as he hurried outside, leaving her alone with the two strange vampires studying her. She swallowed nervously as she tried to shove aside her rising turmoil. "I should grab my things too," she said hurriedly.

She quickly scooted past Annabelle and Liam, feeling only a little guilty about leaving them to fend for themselves. She needed a few minutes to herself in order to gather her scattered thoughts and swaying emotions. She had packed two suitcases already, but she still had to gather her toiletries.

Heading into the bathroom, she began tossing things into her small travel case. She tried not to think as she moved, but all of her doubts and insecurities reared back to life. Zipping the case closed, she slid down to sit on the edge of the tub. Why hadn't he told her about the mate thing?

"Cassie." She lifted her head when Devon appeared in her doorway. "What's wrong?"

She hesitated, unsure of how much to say to him. But in the end, her curiosity and doubts won out. "Why didn't you tell me about the mate thing?"

He sighed as he moved into the room. "It's not the reason you're thinking."

"And how would you know what I'm thinking?" she retorted.

The grin he gave her only caused her irritation to crank up another notch. "Because I know you," he whispered. "You wear your emotions on your face, and I know how you think. I didn't tell you about it because I didn't think you were my mate, because I *know* you are. The reason I didn't tell you was because it is only one more thing for you to be troubled about. It's only one more pressure you do *not* need right now. Your safety is the *only* thing I can be concerned about now."

Cassie stared at him as he knelt before her and took hold of her hands. His eyes burned into hers, the need in them nearly broke her heart. "How can you be so sure I am?" she asked.

He gave her a wry grin as he leaned forward on the balls of his feet. "I've known since the second I saw you, I may not have admitted it to myself then, but I *knew* then. And there was something else..." his voice trailed off, his eyes fell from hers.

"Something else?" she prodded when he didn't continue.

He rose to his feet and settled himself on the tub beside her.

"I've never used my ability for mind control over you Cassie, at least not on purpose."

For a moment she couldn't find her breath. What was he talking about? He had taken control of her mind? Chills raced up and down her spine, he wouldn't look at her. "What do you mean?" she croaked.

His head came up and his eyes finally focused on her again. "There was a night, a time when my ability went beyond my control, while I was sleeping. It sought out your mind and ensnared it in a dream..."

Cassie's hand flew to her mouth as she recalled the dreams she'd had about Devon, and there had been so many of them before she'd accepted him into her life. But out of all the dreams, there had been one so vivid, so *real* it had haunted her. That it had all but driven her into his arms. "The lake," she breathed.

"Yes, the lake."

"It was so real." Cassie's fingers brushed against her lips. It had been the first time she'd ever kissed him, and though it had been amazing, it had been nothing compared to the real thing. "Why?"

"I didn't do it on purpose Cass; I promise you I would never do it on purpose, not to you. If I was ever going to do it on purpose you would have been out of this town months ago, and we never would have been apart for two weeks." Cassie hated the reminder of the weeks they'd spent apart, and how awful she'd been to him. "I think I was growing so frustrated of your continuous refusal of me that it seeped out in my sleep."

He bumped her knee and squeezed her hand. "The hunt was growing tiresome," he said teasingly, though she could hear the strain in his voice. "I went to sleep that night and my power sought you out. It did so because even though I didn't realize it until after I awoke, my subconscious recognized you as my mate, and it had to connect to you in some way. I didn't know I was in your dream until you told me you'd spent your summers there as a child."

Cassie's fingers fell away from her mouth. She could only stare at him, barely able to move, barely able to breathe as he turned toward her. His eyes were intense, his gaze steady and yet fearful. "That's when I knew you were my mate. Don't get me wrong, I continued to try and deny it. I did *not* want you placed in that situation; I didn't want you to know what I was, what my world consisted of. I had no way of knowing you already knew far more of my world than I'd ever suspected."

He leaned forward and clasped her face between his palms. Cassie relished his touch and feel, and the words he spoke. "And after I finally admitted it to myself, finally allowed myself to acknowledge you were my mate, I didn't want to tell you."

"Why?"

His fingers brushed over her face. "Because, I would like you to make the choice to join me on your own without any pressure from me or because you feel obligated."

"And now that I have, it may be impossible," she whispered morosely.

His head bowed, his forehead pressed against hers. "Once you're safe, and all of this is past us, then we can sort out the rest of the details, and we will Cassie. I promise you, we will."

She nodded as she blinked back the tears burning her eyes. She wished she could make this all different or that she'd made the choice earlier. Maybe if she had she could have been turned by now. Maybe, just maybe there would have been no ill effect, and the bond between them could have been forged.

But then again, something awful may have happened. She could have become a monster, and Devon never would have

forgiven himself, even if he'd been unaware of the consequences at the time. No, as awful as it was, it was a good thing
she hadn't made the choice earlier.

"Yes, we will," she agreed. She frowned at him as a new
thought took root inside of her. "Devon, with what Annabelle
described, wouldn't you and Isla be mates?"

His hands constricted on hers. "No Cassie, there is more to it
than just blood and sex. The bond is also forged through love.
There was never any love with Isla, it was never like that. It has
never been like that with anyone but you. Once I turned Isla, I
never shared blood with her again and mates tend to share blood
on a daily basis."

"I see," she said. His gaze was doubtful and questioning.
"I do."

He managed a small smile for her as he wrapped his hand
around the back of her head. He pulled her against him for a
demanding kiss that robbed her of all sense and reason. She lost
herself to the feel of him as he swept away all of her doubts and
concerns. She matched the frantic need of his kiss, knowing this
may be the last time they were alone together for a while.

She didn't realize she was crying until he pulled away and
tenderly wiped the tears from her face. "Don't cry," he whispered as he kissed her cheeks.

"I'm going to miss you so much," she said, unable to keep
the hitching sob from her voice.

He kissed her again and rested his forehead against hers. "I'll
join you as soon as I can," he vowed.

She swallowed heavily. "You'd better, and you'd better stay
safe."

"I will Cassie, don't worry about me, you have to take care
of yourself."

"Of course I worry about you. I love you."

He grinned at her and kissed her again before pulling away. "I love you too. Melissa and Luther are here."

He waited as she threw her travel bag into her suitcase. "Devon." He paused in the doorway with her suitcases as he turned back to her. She swiftly moved toward him and threw her arms around him as she kissed him forcefully. Her suitcases thudded to the floor as he wrapped his arms around her and pressed her against him.

CHAPTER THIRTEEN

CASSIE LISTENED as the trees clicked and creaked with the sway of the breeze shifting through the large maples and oaks. Aside from the noise of the trees, the night was eerily quiet. Picking up her coffee, she held it between her chilled hands as she took a small sip. Chris sat behind her, his feet propped up on the banister, and his hands folded into the sleeves of his parka.

Melissa stepped onto the wraparound porch with a blanket wrapped around her shoulders. The screen door squeaked as she eased it closed. Though it had snowed throughout most of the day, the sky was clear, the stars bright in the dark sky. The moon shimmered over the pristine blanket of white snow. It was one of the most hauntingly beautiful and lonely things Cassie had ever seen.

"It's so peaceful," Melissa murmured.

It *was* peaceful, too peaceful, and Cassie hated it. She missed being part of the action, missed the hustle of her small town and her life. She greatly missed Devon; every fiber of her being ached for him every second of the endlessly long days and nights. She hadn't slept more than two hours at a time since they'd parted last week. Her skin felt like fire ants were crawling over it.

The vibration in her pocket drew her attention to her phone. Her hands trembled in anticipation as she pulled it out. Cassie flipped it open and quickly scanned through Devon's text. He checked in with her as often as he could while searching for Julian. She had to know he was safe; otherwise she would go insane in this cabin, in the middle of nowhere, in upstate Maine. It had every new luxury she could dream of, but the cabin was remote, lonely, and much too far from Devon.

She typed a quick response to him and flipped the phone closed. She held it close, unwilling to lose the small connection the phone gave her to him. Tears burned her eyes as she slid it into her pocket. She hated living apart from him and feeling like this. She hated the uncertainty of both of their futures. And she really hated being taken out of the fight and hidden away.

Movement to the right caught her attention as Annabelle emerged from the woods. She glided gracefully through the almost knee high snow. Her hair shimmered in the glow of the moon as she moved. She wasn't as beautiful as Isla had been, not in the seductive mysterious sense anyway, but she was delicate, pretty and so open and loving it was impossible not to like her.

Though she didn't like it, Cassie fully understood why Devon had thought he was in love with her.

"Couldn't sleep?" Annabelle inquired as she strode soundlessly up the porch steps.

"No," Melissa answered.

Annabelle stomped the snow from her boots. She had a glow about her Cassie recognized as a sign of having fed well. "Where are Dani and Luther?"

"Dani's sleeping, I think. And Luther..." Melissa shrugged as she adjusted the blanket. "He hasn't left his books for more than a catnap and a pee break since we got here."

They'd all spent a lot of time buried amongst the musty books Luther had brought with him, but Luther had been nearly inseparable from the pile. As the pile grew smaller, so did their hopes of finding any answers.

"Hmm," Annabelle murmured.

"Want some coffee?" Chris asked.

Annabelle shook her head so that her long curls bounced around her shoulders. "No, not right now, thank you though."

Cassie nodded, her hands constricted around her cup as she turned back to the hushed night. "Devon and Liam are ok."

Annabelle grinned at her as she clapped her mittens together. "Of course they are, I would know if something happened to Liam."

They all gazed questioningly at her as she continued to clap her hands. "How?" Chris's chair hit the floor of the porch as he dropped his legs down.

Annabelle continued to smile reassuringly. "We share blood; we're connected in that way. I would know if that connection was severed."

A small chill ran through Cassie as she thought over Annabelle's words. "So you would know if something happened to Devon also," she muttered.

Annabelle's eyes were kind and understanding as she turned to Cassie. Cassie hated that look in her eyes, hated the pity she saw there. "It's been years, my blood connection with Devon is much weaker now, but yes, I think I would know."

Cassie nodded as she wrapped her arms around herself as the loneliness inside her grew. She could feel tears burning her eyes and she tried to bat them back. Normally she wouldn't be this emotional, but she'd been uncomfortable in her own skin for the past week.

"You would know also," Annabelle said.

Cassie shook her head. "We don't have that kind of connection," she whispered.

Annabelle frowned as she shook back her bouncing curls. "No, yours is deeper. You would know Cassie, believe me."

Cassie managed a small nod, but she didn't feel reassured. The door opened again as Luther stepped onto the porch. His eyes were bloodshot and weary, his hair a disheveled mess. "Break time?" Melissa inquired.

Luther nodded as he pulled off his glasses and cleaned them on the edge of his shirt. "Have you heard from Devon?"

Cassie frowned thoughtfully as a small surge of hope flipped her heart over. "Yes, have you learned something?"

Luther shook his head as he slipped his glasses back on. "No. I was simply curious if The Commission may have appeared in town yet."

"He hasn't said anything about them, but then again, he hasn't really seen anyone. Not even Julian."

Luther's forehead furrowed as he stared into the distance. "I'm going to have to go back tomorrow to gather some more books."

Cassie's heart lurched as her pulse picked up. "I'll go with you," she blurted as the thought of seeing Devon eased some of the torment in her body.

Luther shook his head no; his eyes were caring but resolved as they met hers. "Absolutely not Cassie," he said firmly.

"But you should have help!"

"Melissa can come with me."

Cassie glanced between them as frustration boiled through her. "I can go!" she retorted.

Luther shook his head firmly. "No Cassie, if The Commission happens to show up, they can't see you. As of now they may know of you, but they have no idea what you look like."

"But they aren't there!" she protested vehemently.

"We don't know that Cassie; they could be hiding. They could also arrive at any time. You have to stay hidden."

Cassie opened her mouth to protest and then closed it. It would be pointless; he wouldn't allow her to go. If she insisted upon it, he would stay here and it was essential they had more books. No matter how useless the books seemed right now, it was the only source of hope she had in these lonely mountains. They were one of the few things keeping her from going completely insane.

Her heart lurched as tears burned her eyes again. "Ok," she reluctantly agreed. "Will you see Devon?"

"Yes."

Despite her best intentions a tear slid free. She wiped it hastily away, if she wasn't careful she would turn into a sobbing mess. She longed to see him, to touch him, and to know he was safe. Her phone vibrated again; she pulled it out to find Devon's reassuring message that he was still safe and everything was fine. More tears slid free.

"Cassie." She looked up as Melissa wrapped her arm around her shoulder and enfolded her in the blanket. "It will be over soon."

"I know."

"Come on let's go inside, it's getting chilly out here. Plus, I think we could use a distraction, maybe a game of cards or Scrabble," Annabelle said with a false cheeriness in her voice.

Chris snorted as he launched to his feet. "Or how about I just kick all your asses on the Wii?"

Cassie couldn't help but grin at him as he strolled by and nudged her shoulder. "Dream on," she retorted.

~

DEVON WATCHED as the Caddy pulled into the driveway. He didn't think Cassie was with them, but he couldn't suppress the small glimmer of hope filling him. Melissa and Luther climbed out of the vehicle and stretched their legs and backs. His spirits crashed when he realized Luther had listened to him and hadn't brought Cassie.

He opened the door for them as they stepped onto the porch. They both offered him tired smiles as they trudged inside. "How was the drive?" he inquired as he closed the door behind them.

"Fine," Luther answered. "How are things going here?"

"I'm beginning to wonder if Julian's still in the area. Maybe Cassie killing Isla scared him off, instead of making him more determined," Devon told him.

Luther lifted an eyebrow. "Do you really believe that?"

"I don't know what to believe," he admitted. "I haven't felt his presence in a while; there was only one new murder and that was the night after you left. I think he suspected there was something off with Cassie, something different. He stopped me from helping her that night..."

"He did what?" Luther interrupted.

Devon paced anxiously as he told Luther what Julian had said and done. Luther stared at him with his eyes as round as an owl's behind his glasses. Melissa's mouth was pinched but she showed no other reaction as she stood rigidly by the door. "What does that mean?" Melissa asked when Devon was done speaking.

"I don't know," Devon answered. "I don't know if it means

he took off after seeing what she'd done to Isla, but I doubt it. I think he would have become more intrigued and he would have tried to test her boundaries as much as possible to see what she was capable of. Or at least the Julian I've always known would have, and I'm not inclined to think he's changed any."

Luther pulled his glasses off and cleaned them as he stared at the floor. "You don't think he followed us out of town?"

"I wouldn't still be here if I did. No, he didn't follow her. I would have known if he had, and Annabelle would have sensed him by now. He is strong, but not strong enough to keep himself cloaked from her and Chris for that long. Besides, there was that one other murder the night after you left."

They shifted uneasily as they glanced toward the door. "Maybe he is laying low in the hopes Cassie will return to town."

Melissa said the words, but he could tell she didn't believe them. "Maybe," he agreed, though he didn't believe it either. However there was no other explanation for Julian's sudden disappearance, or at least not a better one than Melissa had offered. Besides, there was something he was more concerned about at the moment. "How is Cassie doing?"

"As well as can be expected, I guess," Luther mumbled.

Melissa frowned as she folded her arms and her gaze moved over the house. Devon had given up his apartment; he preferred to take up residence in Cassie's home in order to keep an eye on Chris's mom. He also felt closer to Cassie in her home, he could still smell her here, still touch the things that meant so much to her. "Melissa?" he asked.

Her onyx eyes met his, her mouth pressed into a compressed line. "She's miserable," she admitted. "Cassie can take a lot, but she's had more shoved at her in the past month then *anyone* should ever have to handle. She's lost, she's confused, and she needs you."

Devon blinked in surprise, startled to hear Melissa speak so openly about Cassie's emotions and what she was going through. He was also wounded by the truth and heartache resonating behind her words. "Melissa," Luther said reproachfully.

Melissa waved a slender hand. "I know this is what has to be done. It just sucks," she muttered.

Devon thought that summed it up perfectly. "But she'll be ok, right?" he pressed.

"Yes," Melissa answered. "She asked me to give you this."

Melissa pulled a letter from her pocket and handed it over to him. Devon caught the lingering scent of Cassie upon it as he fingered the white envelope before slipping it into his pocket. He wished it was her he was holding, but until this mess was cleared up that wasn't to be. "Thank you. Did you get more books?"

Luther nodded, but he didn't look happy. "There's slim hope of them telling us anything Devon."

Devon ran a hand through his disordered hair. "I know. The few I have here are useless, but there is still *some* hope."

"I suppose so."

The sound of Liam's footsteps turned their heads to the stairs. Liam smiled as he stepped off the stairs; his hair was tussled and still damp from his shower. "How is Annabelle?" he inquired.

"Good," Luther answered. "I think everyone else is starting to go a little stir crazy though."

Liam grinned. "I imagine so."

"You staying the night?" Devon asked.

Luther nodded as he glanced briefly at Melissa. "Neither of us is ready for another seven hours in the car."

"Don't blame you. Want some dinner?"

"Sounds good."

Devon turned to move into the kitchen when he noticed Melissa had frozen. She was as inflexible as a block of ice, her face slack, and her eyes distant and unseeing. A chill of apprehension raced down his spine, the hair on the back of his neck stood on end. He reached for her, but Luther seized hold of his arm.

Luther's face was taut; his eyes callous as he shook his head at Devon. "Cassie," Devon whispered.

Melissa inhaled loudly; staggering back, she hit the wall before she fell to the floor. The horror in her eyes confirmed his worst fear.

CASSIE GLANCED up from her book. The sun filtering through the bare branches cast dancing shadows across the snow covered ground. She didn't know what had caught her attention until she realized the woods had gone completely still. The squirrels no longer moved about in the trees, the birds had all stopped singing.

A chill began to make its way through her, a chill that had nothing to do with the cold day. Slowly, frightened any sudden movement might draw an attack, Cassie placed the book down. She studied the woods as her eyes rapidly darted over the thick trees. Nothing moved amongst the shadowy interior.

The creak of the door caught her attention as Dani came onto the porch. "What are you doing?" she asked quietly.

"I was reading, but..."

"But what?" Dani inquired when Cassie broke off.

"But something's not right," she answered. "We should go back inside. Where are Chris and Annabelle?"

Dani glanced around the woods. "Chris is playing a video game, and I think Annabelle is still sleeping."

Cassie stood and edged toward Dani. "Are you sure something is out there Cassie? It is the day."

"Not all of our enemies are the undead. Go on Dani, get inside."

Cassie edged toward the door, nudging Dani as she moved. In her pocket she felt her phone begin to vibrate. Keeping her eyes on the woods, she pulled it out of her pocket, relieved to see Devon's name on the screen. "Hello," she greeted.

"Where are you?" the growled demand made her skin crawl.

"I'm at the cabin, of course," she said nonchalantly as she tried to keep her alarm from him.

"You have to get Chris and Annabelle, and get out of there now. *Right* now."

Melissa must be with him, she must have had a vision, and if Melissa had a vision...

Cassie shuddered again as her hand squeezed the phone. If Melissa had received a vision, then it was probably already too late. Cassie tried not to panic; Melissa's visions had been thwarted before, it was possible this one could be stopped too.

"Devon." Terror choked her voice as his words completely sank in. Or, actually, his lack of a single name. A sudden knowledge dawned over her and left her hollow and shaken. She realized now there had been one name he hadn't mentioned. Closing her eyes she took a deep, calming breath. "I love you."

"Cassie..."

His words were cut off as she spun suddenly and launched at Dani. She realized only too late her mistake. She should have gone the other way, should have tried to get off the porch instead of confronting Dani head on. Dani had been prepared for Cassie, whereas Cassie hadn't been prepared for her.

The jolt from the taser gun slammed into her shoulder and knocked her back a good five feet before she fell into the wall. Her body jerked with spasms as bolts of electricity pounded into her. Pain exploded through her, blood filled her mouth as she bit down on her tongue.

The jolts suddenly stopped. Cassie slumped to the ground, unable to move as her body went limp. Her fingers clawed at the wood of the porch, she tried to form a coherent word, tried to get her body to move again, but her limbs simply wouldn't cooperate with her frazzled mind. She couldn't gather her wits enough to feel the outrage she knew she should feel.

She couldn't summon the sense of betrayal that should be directed at Dani. An anger that would give her the power, and ability, to get up and moving again if she experienced enough of it. She didn't have the strength to ponder what was going on, or how Dani was involved with this.

No, she could only sit helpless in her tortured, frazzled body.

Her eyes rolled as movement caught her attention. Figures began to emerge from the woods. Her head lolled to the side as four men climbed the stairs of the porch. Dani handed the taser gun over to the first man, who gave her a brisk nod.

"Good job. The others?"

"They've been taken care of."

Cassie uttered a garbled moan as her heart constricted. Taken care of? What did that mean? Taken care of *how*? Fear for her friend's safety gave her a new strength. She lurched forward as she tried to regain her footing in a desperate attempt to break free. She had barely moved a foot before a fresh bolt of electricity slammed her backward.

Her legs kicked spasmodically; blood from her chomped tongue spurted from her mouth as a choked cry escaped her. "You were right, she is tougher than we'd thought," another man said. "Two taser shots and she's still trying to get up. Tranquilize her."

Another cry escaped as they came at her with a syringe in hand. Cassie tried to get the strength to move, but her limp legs and arms refused to cooperate with her. Hands seized hold of her and pinned her against the wall. A shrill, unintelligible noise escaped her as the needle jabbed into her arm and the plunger was pushed.

CHAPTER FOURTEEN

CHRIS WOKE to the feel of tiny hands scrambling over him as they tugged at something. He groaned as he cracked an eyelid. He was surprised to find Annabelle kneeling before him, her delicate nose scrunched in frustration. He blinked as he tried to figure out what was going on, and just what she was pulling at.

His throat was unnaturally dry. His tongue felt funny, and was that burnt hair he smelled? He swallowed heavily to wet his parched throat in order to find words. What had happened? His gaze shot to the video game he'd been playing. The screen was still on, his car was crashed into a wall and a prompter asked if he planned to continue. The only thing he intended to do was figure out what was going on.

Annabelle grunted in frustration and then jerked hard on something. Chris's hand went with her. He was surprised to see a rope falling away from his wrist. "What..." the word came out as a croak. He swallowed heavily as Annabelle's sea colored eyes came up to his. The terror in her gaze was almost enough to make him lose his voice again. "What happened?"

Annabelle tugged at his other hand and freed the last rope keeping his arm in place. "Dani happened."

"Excuse me?" he choked out.

Annabelle nodded as she rose. She kept her hand on Chris's arm as she grabbed a can of soda from the table. She thrust it at him and studied him apprehensively as he took a small sip. "How are you feeling?"

Chris shook his head, grateful for the drink. His mind rapidly cleared, but he was beginning to wish it hadn't. "Where's Cassie?"

Annabelle shook her head. "Gone."

"Gone? Gone where?" he demanded, nearly spilling his soda as he lurched forward.

"I don't know," she whispered. "We've been out for hours Chris. They could have taken her anywhere by now."

Chris's heart pounded against his ribs with the force of a jackhammer. He stumbled up, and nearly tripped over the video game controller that had fallen at his feet. Annabelle steadied him before he could take a header through the flat screen. Panic caused his temples to throb with the rush of his blood.

"We have to find her! What happened?" he nearly bellowed.

"Chris calm down," Annabelle urged. "Please, just calm down, we have to think. We have to figure out who came here, who took her."

"I don't know what happened, one minute I was playing a game, and the next you were untying me from this chair!"

His voice reverberated loudly around the room. He took a deep breath as he tried to calm himself but failed miserably. Cassie was gone; someone, or some*thing*, had taken her. He cursed viciously as he slammed his fist on the table. His soda rattled, some of it splashed over the side, but everything remained standing.

"Feel better?" Annabelle asked.

No, he felt like an idiot, torn and tormented. He felt like tearing this house down, then the woods, and then whatever else he could get his hands on, but none of that would do them any good. He took another deep breath, as he ran his hand through his hair and tried to steady himself.

He didn't understand where the full force of this panic and anger was coming from. Yes, he should be terrified, and upset, but *this* bad...

His thoughts trailed off as realization dawned on him. It wasn't him who felt like ripping the house down, or the woods, or everything in his way. It was *Devon*. Devon was near, and his emotions were so strong, and so forceful, he was picking up on them, and being affected by them. His skin became flushed as a cold chill swept down his spine.

"Devon's almost here," he told her.

Annabelle's eyes widened, her mouth parted as she glanced at the window. "How bad is he?"

"Bad," Chris whispered.

Annabelle turned back to him and her hands fisted. "Chris, I think you should go somewhere else, at least until he calms down. He's going to be on a rampage, and he's not going to care who is in his way."

Chris gaped at her, aghast at the thought. "I'm not hiding from him," he informed her.

"It's not hiding Chris, but he isn't going to be controllable, and if you get in his way we may not be able to stop him. When a vampire's mate is threatened, or lost to them, they don't think rationally. What is going to come through that door is not the Devon you know. What is going to come through that door will destroy anyone who gets in between him and Cassie."

"Well, we aren't in between them," Chris grated. "And I'm

not leaving you alone with him."

"I'm sure Liam is with him. Maybe even the others still."

Chris tried to sort through Devon's emotions to see if there were others with him, but it was impossible to tell beneath all of the fury. Devon's emotions threatened to bury him beneath their sucking tidal wave. He'd thought Devon's misery and anguish had been bad when Cassie broke up with him, but this was far *far* worse. This bordered on the edge of insanity.

"He's going to kill us all," Chris whispered, suddenly convinced of it. Devon was strong enough, and savage enough right now to destroy them without batting an eyelash. He could kill hundreds of people before someone ever stopped him. If someone, other than Cassie, even could.

Annabelle's delicate jaw was set and her sea green eyes hardened. "If Cassie is still alive, we have a chance of reaching him. If she *is* dead, then there will be no stopping him. A vampire without their mate is as good as dead."

"She has to be alive," Chris said. "She *has* to be."

"Do you know that for sure?"

Chris shook his head; the only thing he knew for sure was he wasn't ready to face the loss of his best friend, or the loss of his own life for that matter. "No, I don't, but even…" he broke off. "Even if she is dead, I thought they didn't complete the ritual. I mean Cassie is still human. They aren't mates, right?"

Annabelle had made her way over to the window. "He still recognizes her as his mate. He still knows in his heart she *is* his. He cannot live without her, Chris."

"Will he know if she is still alive if the bond wasn't completed?"

"For our sakes, let's hope so," she whispered.

"He's here."

Annabelle stepped away from the window. The luminosity

of the moon and the television cast an eerie glow about the living room that did little to ease the chill taking up residence inside him. Over Annabelle's shoulder he could see a figure emerging from the woods, moving with so much speed it was a blur amongst the trees. Chris took an involuntary step back as he tried to avoid the frenzy emanating from the blur.

"Where's Liam?" he whispered.

"He's not as fast as Devon." Annabelle moved closer to Chris and stepped in front of him.

Footsteps sounded on the porch. Chris braced himself as the steps hesitated before stomping into the house. Devon's ferocity pounded against him as he made his way into the foyer and his silhouette appeared in the doorway. He held something in his hand and his head was bowed over it. For a single moment he fingered it before lifting his head to look at them.

Chris inhaled sharply as Devon's blood red eyes narrowed upon them. Annabelle straightened her shoulders, but Chris could feel her fear. "Where is she?" Devon demanded.

"Devon, you have to calm down," Annabelle urged.

He took a step into the room. "*Who* took her?"

"Devon..."

"Who Annabelle?" he bellowed so loudly the windows shook.

Annabelle jumped and pushed Chris back as she moved away. "That is what we must figure out," she said calmly. "But I believe it was The Commission."

Chris glowered at her. He didn't like being associated with anything, or any*one*, who may have had something to do with Cassie's disappearance. Unfortunately, The Commission was something he *could* be associated with. Devon was irrational right now; he might blame Chris for Cassie's disappearance.

"Devon look, we need to figure this out. If you could just

calm down, we may be able to trace her location. Her blood is inside of you." Chris was riveted by shock. Cassie had allowed Devon to feed from her? He didn't know why he was so surprised; it made sense for them to crave that connection after all. He just hadn't suspected it had happened already. "I know you've fed from her. I can smell it, and sense it, in the power radiating from you. That power is also making you more irrational now."

Another blur caught Chris's attention before fresh footsteps hit the porch. Liam appeared behind Devon and his silver eyes instantly latched upon Annabelle. Though Chris had been afraid to move an inch, Liam strode past Devon as he hurried to Annabelle's side. Chris could sense their longing for each other, but they didn't touch as Liam reached her side.

"We, all of *us*, we can find her Devon," Annabelle continued gently. "With all of our gifts..."

"Before they hurt her?" Devon demanded. "Can we find her *before* they hurt her?"

"We can find her. If she is still alive, we can find her. And she is alive, right Devon?"

Chris could read the truth in the easing of Devon's features, Cassie was alive. His best friend had not been lost, yet. There was still time to get her back. Hopefully before Devon went completely insane.

Headlights filtered over the windows and tires crunched in the snow. Doors opened and slammed, running footsteps sounded over the driveway and then up the steps. Melissa and Luther burst through the door and skidded to a halt when Devon turned wrath fueled eyes on them. Luther shoved Melissa back a step, Liam moved instinctively closer to them.

"Devon please come in and sit down," Annabelle coaxed. "Please."

Devon didn't move. He remained standing like an opposing avenger sent straight from the depths of Hell. Chris only prayed he wouldn't turn that wrath upon them, though he still appeared very close to doing so. "No. Tell me what happened here," Devon commanded.

Annabelle looked around helplessly. "At least let me turn on some lights. Let us get comfortable, so we can try to formulate a game plan."

Annabelle moved away as she hedged toward the switch by Devon. Liam bristled beside Chris, but didn't move to go after her as she neared Devon. The lights flared on, causing everyone to blink in surprise. "What happened?" Liam inquired as he glanced around the living room.

Chris took note of the rope on the floor by the chair where he'd been tied. He glanced at the bowl of soup he'd eaten shortly before utter blackness had claimed him. A bowl of soup *Dani* had made for him.

"Dani happened," he muttered as Annabelle's words finally sank in. He hadn't known what to make of her statement earlier, but now, with nausea twisting through his belly, he completely understood what she'd been trying to say. "*Dani* did this."

"Yes," Melissa said flatly. "She did."

Chris frowned at her as he sensed more behind her words. "You had a vision?"

Melissa nodded briskly. "Too late though, they're almost always too late!" she spat.

"But what exactly did she do?" Chris demanded. "I was playing the video game, and next thing I know I was waking up tied to a freaking chair! And why? *Why* did she do this?"

"I think there was something in your soup," Annabelle answered. "Some kind of drug, you were out cold when I got down here."

"Where were you?" Liam inquired though the tension in his voice belied his quiet tone.

Annabelle ducked her head as her long lashes fell to cover her eyes. "Upstairs," she admitted. "Dani came into my room, and we were talking. She said she was scared, confused," Annabelle's delicate forehead furrowed as she tried to recall the conversation. "I remember giving her a hug, and then nothing. I was tied to the bed when I woke up, the hair on my arms was still slightly singed."

"She electrocuted you," Liam grated.

Chris took a small step away from him. They already had one very pissed off vampire to deal with, they didn't need another one. Annabelle nodded. "I believe so."

Liam let out a low growl. Annabelle went to him and took hold of his hand as she turned toward Melissa. "What did your vision show you?"

Melissa shot an anxious look at Devon, who was watching her raptly, his eyes cold and furious. Chris was certain Devon had already heard the answer to this, but he wasn't going to stop her from the retelling. "Dani tasered Cassie. I saw her go down, and then four men came out to retrieve her."

Devon swore furiously, he spun on his heel as he paced away. Melissa and Luther took that as their chance to slip by him and join the others in the living room. "The men?" Chris asked.

"Were out in the daytime, they were human. I'm almost positive they were part of The Commission."

Devon swore again as his pacing became more agitated. "Why would Dani do this?" Chris asked.

"I don't know," Luther answered. "Maybe it has something to do with her brother, but I don't know. We have no idea what happened to her, or what she did, before we met her."

"I know what will happen to her when I'm done with her," Devon snarled as he stopped in the doorway again.

The hair on Chris's arms stood on end. He'd seen Devon out of control, feral. It had always been when Cassie was threatened, but this was... well this was different. Devon *would* destroy Dani; if he found her he *would* kill her. Chris wasn't too fond of the girl anymore either, but what Devon would do to her was something he didn't want to imagine, or see.

Then, suddenly, those malevolent red eyes were locked upon him. "You didn't sense anything from her?" Devon demanded.

Chris swallowed heavily. "No, nothing like this."

"What *did* you sense then?"

"Fear, confusion," he said. "I sensed no betrayal in her, no animosity, nothing deceitful or mean."

"How could you not?" Devon demanded.

Chris took a deep breath as he tried to puzzle that out for himself. "It's stronger when I touch a person. I can always read their emotions and inner personality better then. But now that I think about it, I haven't touched Dani in a long time. I never questioned it at the time, never realized it until now, but she must have stayed away from me on purpose. Also, yours and Cassie's emotions have been running so high lately it's been difficult for anything else to get through. Especially here, Cassie was a jumbled mess of confusion and loneliness while she was here. What I sensed from Dani was nothing compared to that."

For a second Chris was certain Devon was going to fly across the room and rip his head off. Chris knew he was quite capable of doing it. Swallowing heavily, Chris took a small step back but it would do him little good. If Devon was determined to get a hold of him, he would.

"I thought you could block out people's emotions," Melissa said.

Chris looked helplessly at her. "Not when they're so strong like that. Their emotions get through anyway, no matter how much I try to block them out. In all honesty, I trusted Dani; I never sensed any animosity or ill will from her before. I never thought to search her anytime recently; there was no reason to doubt her."

"Ok, so none of us saw this coming," Annabelle interjected.

"Until it was too late," Melissa muttered in disgust.

Chris squeezed her shoulder reassuringly. "We have to find out where they took her," Luther said. "And why she's still alive."

Chris inhaled as he shot Luther a ferocious look. He loved the man, but sometimes he could be completely obtuse. "What do you mean *why* she is still alive?" Devon's voice was so low and menacing everyone took a small step back from him.

Luther, realizing his mistake, cleared his throat nervously. Chris fervently hoped he would change the subject, or at least think of some way to cover his words. Unfortunately, Luther didn't possess those social skills. "They came for her because of what type of Hunter she is. We'd assumed they killed off the other Hunters like her, but if they took Cassie alive we may have been mistaken. They may have been doing something else with those Hunter's, we just don't know what."

Stunned silence followed his statement. Chris waited with bated breath for Devon's reaction, which he was sure was going to be violent. He wasn't disappointed. A loud bellow ripped from Devon as he seized hold of the hall table near him. Lifting it, he swung it easily up and slammed it into the wall with enough force to shatter the table and plaster. They all instinctively ducked as plaster exploded in bits of white powder, and table pieces flew outward.

Devon stood amongst the ruined debris, his shoulders heaving, his fists clenched so firmly the muscles and veins in his arms stood out starkly. Though he looked on the verge of tearing the whole place down, he didn't move to destroy anything else. "Nice Luther," Melissa scolded.

He shot her a severe glance. "There is no sugarcoating this," he replied. "We need to figure out what is going on, where she is, and we have to do it quickly. As long as she is alive, Devon *will* hold himself together."

Chris didn't care to think about what would happen if Cassie didn't *stay* alive. He had grown close to Devon, had started to consider him one of his good friends, but if Cassie died that Devon would cease to exist. And this Devon would take over completely. The *man* would be destroyed as the demon inside rushed forth to take control. Chris shuddered as he realized there was a good possibility he may lose two of his best friends. That he may have to destroy one of them himself, if Devon didn't destroy all of them first.

"So let's find her," Liam said. "Devon can you track her through her blood?"

Devon stood rigidly for a minute, his hands uncurling as he seemed to regain some control of himself. When he turned to them though, his eyes were still the color of rubies. "No. I picked her scent up again when we were miles away. It came here, and then it just stopped."

"That makes no sense," Annabelle murmured.

"He picked up the trail on what would have been their way out," Liam explained. "Where he started is also where we lost her."

"That still shouldn't happen," Annabelle insisted. "I know where Liam is at all times, I could find him anywhere. You should be able to find her."

"Our bond isn't complete Annabelle!" Devon grated. "Cassie

doesn't have my blood in her, and although I have hers, the bond isn't strong enough for me to follow her."

Chris looked at Luther and Melissa to see how they would react to his statement. Both of their faces remained impassive, but Melissa glanced quickly over at him and he could feel her surprise. She hadn't known what had transpired between Devon and Cassie either, but he was fairly certain Luther had, or he had at least suspected it.

"But you can't follow her blood?" Luther inquired.

"Only so far," Devon answered. "They've taken her beyond that point, and it's been so long..."

Devon broke off and shuddered as a trace of humanity slipped through the fright and rage boiling inside of him. Without Cassie, Devon wouldn't survive, and yet Chris sensed no concern for Devon's own life. He only cared about Cassie's. For a moment his eyes turned green again, and then the red shuddered back into place and fury blasted against Chris once more.

"There has got to be a way!" Melissa cried. "There has to be! We can follow her trail until Devon loses it and then we'll just have to..."

Melissa looked helplessly at Chris as tears slipped down her face. Chris understood her helplessness, her complete and utter lack of power. "Liam, what ability do you have?" Luther demanded.

Hope shot through Chris as he turned to Liam. They didn't know what he was capable of, what ability he may possess that could be of use to them right now. "I can communicate with animals, which does us little good in this situation."

Chris started in surprise, it seemed like a handy little gift to him. "Can't we just talk to them; won't they be able to tell us where they took her?"

Liam frowned as he shook back his brown hair. "They may be able to tell us for a little bit, but to find enough of them that have seen something..."

"We need something quicker and easier," Devon interrupted.

Devon emitted a low growl as he paced to the door and then back again. Chris stood quietly as he tried to piece everything together. He needed to think, they had to figure something out before it was too late.

"Julian," he stated.

"What?" Melissa asked in surprise.

"Julian," Chris gushed out. "Julian can find where she is. All we have to do is give him something of Dani's, and he will know everything she knew! He can tell us where to find them!"

Astonished silence met his eager outburst. "Why would he help us?" Annabelle finally asked.

"Because we're going to *make* him," Devon grated out. "We have to gather some of Dani's things."

Before anyone could respond Devon turned and rapidly bounded up the stairs. Chris listened as he threw open doors before finally finding Dani's room. "I'll go help him before he tears the place down," Liam said before he disappeared from the room.

"What if this doesn't work?" Melissa inquired.

"It has to," Luther answered. "It's all we have."

"Did Devon run the whole way here?" Chris asked, more to divert the conversation away from the doubt than out of any real curiosity.

Luther shook his head. "He got out of the vehicle about thirty miles back. That's probably where he picked up her scent."

"If we don't find her, this *will* get ugly," Annabelle whispered. "And I'm fairly certain all of us together won't be enough to take him down."

"No, we're not," Chris agreed.

Melissa squeezed his arm. "We'll find her, I don't care what it takes we *will* find her. Julian will help us."

Chris wanted desperately to believe her, but he was unable to bury the doubts blazing through him. He listened as Devon and Liam pounded back down the stairs. "Let's go," Devon commanded briskly.

"Wait, Devon." Luther held up a hand and took a step forward to intercept Devon before he could leave. "I think we should split up. Liam and I should stay here and search for the animals. It may be a long shot, but it is one we should pursue."

Devon's shoulders became rigid. "Fine."

Annabelle looked about ready to protest as her eyes darted toward Liam. Liam gave a brief shake of his head to forestall her words. "It will be for the best," he said. "Luther can drive while I search the forest, and he can find us places to stay during the day."

"It's settled then, let's go."

Before anyone could say anything more, Devon stormed out of the house. "Liam," Annabelle whispered.

He shook his head as he seized her hand. "You must stay with him, Annabelle, you may be one of the only people who can keep him calm, and I must go. We have to find her before he begins to truly destroy everyone and everything. I will be fine, now go on."

Tears shimmered in Annabelle's eyes as she stood on her toes to kiss him. Chris turned away and followed out the door behind Melissa and Luther. Devon had already disappeared into the forest.

CHAPTER FIFTEEN

A LOW MOAN escaped her as she woke sluggishly. Her entire body ached; her mouth was as dry as a bone. She could barely get her eyes open, and once she did, the light burned them so badly she instantly clamped them shut again. Her groggy mind strained to process what little bits of information she could pick up. She was lying on a bed, a small one, probably a cot. The sheets were cool, and there was only one pillow.

She knew she was far from where she was supposed to be, and that was about all she did know.

Slowly she forced her eyes open again. She blinked against the radiance blazing harshly from the fluorescent fixture in the ceiling. The walls were white concrete. Half of the wall across from her was taken up by a giant piece of one way glass. Her skin crawled at the realization there was probably someone on the other side, watching her.

Gathering her shaking arms beneath her, she managed to shove herself into a sitting position. Her heart lurched in her chest as a thin layer of sweat coated her body. Turning, Cassie's heart thumped faster at the sight of another, smaller window behind her. Her attention turned to the door next to the glass across from her. She knew it would be locked, but she wasn't about to just sit here.

Shoving herself to her feet, she stumbled slightly and almost fell over. She crashed into the wall and winced as pain lanced through her bruised shoulder. Sucking in a deep lungful of air, she tried to ease the dizziness and nausea rolling through her. For a moment she thought she was going to vomit, or pass out. She fought against the darkness trying to pull her under; she most certainly didn't like the idea of being unconscious in this place again.

It took a few minutes before she felt steady enough to move again. She passed by another door cracked open to reveal a small bathroom beyond. Shuffling past the bathroom she made it to the main door. She grabbed hold of the handle, not at all surprised to find it locked. Frustration tore through her as she yanked desperately at the handle.

A small cry of aggravation escaped as she slammed her hand against the door. She rested her forehead on the cool metal as she tried to gather her shaken wits. She didn't scream for help, she knew no one would come, or at least no one she *wanted* to see. Standing on tiptoe, she stared out the small window in the center of the door.

Brilliant beams bounced off the white linoleum floors of the hall. She saw no movement, sensed no sign of a human presence out there. She tried to summon her wrath, to gather the vast strength that had helped her to destroy Isla and might help her get out of this. But it didn't come surging to the forefront. It seemed buried inside of her, trapped by something she had no control over.

She recalled the shot they'd given her. There was a foggy, drugged feeling still clouding her mind. What had they *done* to her? What had they given her? And what was she doing here?

"You're awake."

Cassie jumped back and nearly fell over as she stumbled away from the door. Her gaze flitted around the room as she tried to pinpoint the source of the voice. Her gaze landed on the speakers she hadn't noticed beneath the larger mirror. Illumination suddenly flooded on behind the mirror to reveal the man who had spoken to her. Cassie's mouth dropped, astonishment riveted her as she recognized the man on the other side as Dani's brother, Joey.

She backed away from the mirror until her calves brushed up against the back of the small cot. Her mind was spinning with a million questions, none of which she could actually form into words. Another man moved in to stand beside Joey, Cassie vaguely recognized him as one of the men who had come onto the porch to retrieve her.

"Where am I?" she managed to choke out. "What do you want with me?"

The strange man stepped forward and hit a button to allow him to speak. "You are a menace to people and to your race; we couldn't allow you to be free."

Cassie's mouth dropped open. She glanced around the room as she tried to understand exactly what was going on, and just how bad her situation was. "So you plan on keeping me here to keep others safe?" she demanded.

The men exchanged a look. Joey's auburn hair was the color of blood in the glow of the fluorescents; his pale brown eyes were distant. The man at his side remained impassive. His face was a mask of indifference, his hair neatly trimmed and graying at the edges. His dark blue eyes were as cold as granite. It was the look of speculation and curiosity in his gaze that frightened her most. He stared at her as if she were a bug, something to be picked and prodded at, something he planned to dissect.

Cassie fought to keep her composure as a crushing sense of doom threatened to descend upon her. "No, we have other plans for you," the man answered.

Cassie fisted her hands as she fought the shaking trying to rattle through her. "And what would those plans be?"

"You're a fascinating specimen Cassandra." Cassie shuddered at the word specimen, her stomach twisted with nausea. "There is a lot of power and ability in you. You *did* kill Isla after all, and she was almost an Elder. We are going to try and harness that power, try and use it to our advantage. We do need an advantage desperately. The only problem is you have no control over your abilities."

Confusion swirled through her as she gazed back and forth between them. "You plan on teaching me how to control it?" she managed to grate out.

"No, because we cannot control *you*," he said flatly. "We plan on trying to harness it, on trying to learn from it."

"I don't understand."

"We are losing the war; we need all the weapons we can get. You will be one of those weapons. We just have to learn how to use you in order to make The Hunter race stronger and your blood may be our way to do so."

Cassie's legs gave out as she slid onto the small cot. "You're supposed to be the good guys," she whispered.

"We are, but in every battle innocent lives must be lost. And you are not an innocent Cassandra, consorting with the enemy and all."

"Devon is *not* the enemy!" she snapped. "He's saved my life numerous times, and he is a *good* man!"

"He's a monster," Joey retorted as abhorrence twisted his features. "And you're a disgrace."

"At least I didn't run!" Anger gave her strength to leap to her feet. "I stayed and fought the battle. I stayed and fought the *war*! You ran and hid like the coward you are!"

Joey took a step forward, but he couldn't go any further than the wall before him. "You're a damn *whore*!" he spat at her.

Cassie's hands fisted as some of the anger she'd been searching for came to the forefront. The man rested a hand on Joey's shoulder and pulled him back a step. "You allowed the vampire to feed from you, but I'm assuming you didn't take any of his blood. I'm assuming this exchange didn't occur because the vampire was worried about what it may do to you." Cassie refused to say anything more as she turned her gaze to the ceiling and the strange vents above her. "I also wonder what his blood would do to you."

Terror melted her resolve not to speak again. "You leave him alone!"

Joey groaned as he rolled his eyes. "Quick to defend your lover."

Cassie glared at him. "We don't need him," the other man informed her. "We have something just as good."

A cold chill washed through her, and she was almost forced to sit again as her legs buckled a little. She wouldn't give them the satisfaction of seeing such a weakness in her though. "What do you mean?" she choked out.

The man reached down and flipped another switch. A wash of light flooded from the window behind her. The hair on the back of her neck stood on end as she felt a set of eyes burning into her back. A shudder tore through her. Her mouth was completely dry as she turned slowly.

Julian was standing behind the glass, his arms raised above

his head as he grasped hold of the top of the windowsill. His handsome face was remorseless, his eyes a sadistic shade of red as he stared murderously at the men behind her before his gaze shifted to her. His eyes gradually turned back to their startling ice blue color. Oddly though, the nearly white band around his pupils remained red. It was a startling effect that robbed her of her breath.

"Hello Princess," he purred.

Cassie's breath exploded out of her as she began to tremble all over. What was Julian doing here? And just what did they expect to have happen? There were endless possibilities about what his presence here meant, and none of them were good.

"Julian is also an Elder with some amazing abilities from what I understand," the strange older man informed her with a calm reasoning that shook her. She began to understand the man was truly crazy.

She couldn't find words, could barely find her breath. She slid back to the cot as her legs gave out. "You plan to experiment on us," she whispered.

"We plan to do a lot with you. Now, I would suggest you get some rest; you're going to have a very active day tomorrow."

The light flashed off; Joey and the man disappeared from view. Her hands tightened on the bed as she gasped for air. "Don't breathe too deep."

She turned back to Julian as she struggled not to shed the tears burning her eyes. "What?"

He lifted a dark eyebrow as a small scowl twisted his full mouth. His muscles flexed and bunched as he leaned closer to the window. "Don't breathe too deep; they pump something into these rooms, some kind of tranquilizer. Though I don't particularly require air to breathe, it still gets into my system. It also comes in the blood they give me, as I imagine it will come in your food."

"Oh God," she moaned. She dropped her head as she began to rock back and forth.

"There is no God here, only men trying to play God. Don't fall apart on me princess; we're going to need *you* to get out of here."

She looked up at him in surprise. "Me?" she croaked.

He nodded. "Well, I can't do it alone. With that nifty little getting pissed off and destroying things trick you have, I'm thinking between the two of us we can escape."

Cassie shook her head as she tried to keep her wits through the horror and confusion beating against her. Was she really having a conversation with *Julian* about joining together in something?

Cassie blinked as she fought to rid herself of the awful fogginess, and surreal reality she found herself in. She wanted to deny it, but she knew this was very real, and she was in a lot of trouble, as was Julian. If it meant having to help him to get herself out of here, she would do whatever it took to get back to Devon and her friends. She would do anything she could to escape the madmen now holding her life hostage.

"I can't..." she broke off as she inhaled a shuddery breath. "I tried getting mad already, and I can't. It must be something they gave me, or are still giving me." Her gaze shot to the vents in the ceiling. They were too small for her to crawl out of, but apparently just big enough to constantly pump a stream of tranquilizer into her. "Plus, even if I could get mad, I can't control it. I become something else, something perilous and volatile. Something with no reason or rationality, you don't want that *thing* coming out. There is no way to know what the consequences of it would be."

A loud crash sounded from behind her. Cassie jumped and whirled around as he smashed his hands against the thickly layered glass again. It rattled in the frame, but held firm. Cassie stared at the glass, wondering just how thickly layered it was, and what they had used that could keep a vampire at bay.

Julian's eyes were a scorching red. "I don't give a damn what you become," he snarled. "Without it, we are going to turn into lab rats in here! They are going to poke and prod at us until they are satisfied, and then they are going to kill us. So *princess*," he spat. "You have to tap into that little ability of yours, or we're both going to rot in here. From the sounds of it, what they plan on doing to me is nothing compared to what they plan to do to *you*!"

Cassie's gaze shot back to the thick metal door on the other side; she desperately searched for some way to escape this horrendous situation. But what could she do if she was tranquilized? What help could she possibly be if she couldn't tap into the rage that helped to fuel her strength and agility to higher levels?

She studied the vents again. The ceiling was a good twelve feet high; if she stood on the bed she wouldn't be able to reach it to block the vents somehow. Julian's strong jaw clenched; a muscle jumped in his cheek. His eyes were once more their chilly ice blue, and the bands of nearly white around his pupils were back in place. His normally spiked white blond hair limply hung against his refined features. He was a brutal murderer and a vicious bastard, but she couldn't help but admire his harsh beauty. He was a creature used to getting and taking whatever he wanted, *whenever* he wanted it. He wasn't used to being caged like an animal.

"How long have you been here?" she asked quietly.

His mouth twisted into a snarl, his fangs extended as he turned now blood colored eyes toward the darkened window across from her. "Too long," he grated. "Over a week now, maybe two."

Cassie gaped at him, they'd been hunting him and he'd been locked in here almost the entire time. "But how did you get here?"

"Same way as you I suppose, that little bitch Grounder of yours."

"Dani?" Cassie squeaked as her thoughts turned to Annabelle and Chris. Were they ok? What had Dani done to them? She didn't believe they were in here with her; Dani had said they'd been taken care of. But what exactly did that mean? Had she killed them, or simply left them incapable of trying to defend Cassie?

Cassie fought not to shed the tears burning her eyes. They had to be ok. But as of now, there was absolutely nothing she could do about it, other than hope Dani still had enough decency in her not to harm innocent people. Cassie didn't know how likely that was considering Dani had so easily turned on her.

"How is that possible, Dani was with us?" she whispered.

"I didn't say she was the one who took me," he mumbled. "I'm just assuming she had a hand in it. They knew where I was hunting, knew what my ability was, and knew how to take me. Her brother has one hell of an ability too."

She hoped they weren't listening to them, but she highly doubted it. "Joey? What can he do, and how do you know he's her brother?"

"Yes, Joey," he rumbled. His eyes were intent upon her. "How do you not know what one of your *own* can do?"

Cassie glowered at him. "We didn't all keep in touch after

The Slaughter," she retorted. "Chris and I didn't even know what we were until we were thirteen, and there is no way to know how many Hunters are left out there, never mind what they are capable of."

"Ahh, The Slaughter," Julian's eyes became distant and fond as a small smile curved his mouth. Cassie's temper prickled; a rippling flowed through her at the joy she sensed beneath his words. "Good times."

"Screw you!" she spat. She launched to her knees as a burst of rage flowed through her. "Screw you, you ass!"

Julian's eyes narrowed upon her as a small smile quirked his mouth. Cassie's hands fisted at her sides she wished the glass wasn't between them because she would like to pummel that smug look off his face. "Angry now, Princess?"

Cassie wanted to feel the flash of fury because she was fairly certain she could rip this glass apart to get at him if she did. She felt the slither of anger coiling within her, but the full force of it wouldn't come forth. "What have they done to me?" she whispered.

Julian's hands slid down the window as he knelt before her. She lifted her head to meet his steady gaze. She had expected to see smugness; instead there was understanding, and compassion. Cassie was taken aback as he continued to study her.

"They've drugged you Princess, and like me, you are unable to fully break through the effect of those drugs. I was hoping you would be different, because you *are* different in so many ways, but apparently they have taken that into account."

He sat back on his heels as he ran his hand wearily through his disordered hair. His gaze went to the window behind her. "How did they get you?"

"That little bitch's nut job brother..."

"Joey," she supplied as she stifled a yawn.

He scowled down at her as he folded his thickly muscled arms over his broad chest. "You call him what you want to, and I'll call him what I want to. Nut job has telekinesis, the ability to move things with his mind," he elaborated at her confused look. "Three of them took me down with electricity, and one with a drugged dart. Then *nut job* pinned me down like a freaking bug while the others came forward to drug me further. Freaks."

Cassie was unable to stifle her next yawn. "It's a war remember, you were just enjoying reminiscing about the near destruction of my race. This war has been going on for over a thousand years. I thought you, of all people, would enjoy it."

His eyes darkened as his hands pressed flat against the glass once more. His nose nearly touched the glass as he stared at her. "Wars result in blood and death. If they'd killed me that would be understandable, honorable even, but this is a bloody *freak* show! This is not war; this is a bunch of madmen who have lost their minds."

Cassie sleepily stared up at him as a shiver worked its way through her. He was right; they *were* madmen, and it had been madmen and scientists who created the Hunter line to begin with. Cassie's fingers dug into her arms as she tried to keep herself under control.

"Just like they did before," she mumbled as her eyes shot back to the shadowed glass.

"Yes," Julian agreed. "Just like before, except now *we* are the ones trapped in these cages like rats."

She couldn't help but give him an amused look. "So you would rather be dead then?"

"Wouldn't you?"

Her smile slipped away. A shudder tore through her at the

mere thought of what they might do, of what they were *going* to do to them. Her worst nightmares didn't begin to scratch the surface of what these monsters had in mind for the two of them. She had never truly desired death. There had been a brief period, after her grandmother's death, where she'd considered her life nearly over, and she hadn't been frightened by that. However, she hadn't truly *wanted* to die, no matter how much she'd thought she did. But now, well now she found she might end up vastly preferring death to their current circumstances.

She had only one hope.

"Devon will find us," she whispered.

Julian snorted in disgust. "Keep dreaming, Princess."

Her hands fisted as she rounded on him. "He will come!" she retorted.

He bent down so he was eye level with her. "I have no doubt he *is* looking for you; it is only a matter of *how* is he going to find you?"

She had no idea *how*, but she believed he *would*. There had to be a way, someway, it was the only hope she had, and if she lost that hope she was going to go crazy in this small cell. Swallowing heavily she forced herself to defiantly return his steady stare. "Devon will find a way," she insisted. "Maybe Liam..."

His full mouth curved in amusement as he shook his head. "Liam talks to animals, not much help there. My ability was probably the only hope they did have, and I'm not going to do them much good in here."

Cassie's nostrils flared as she exhaled explosively. Her sudden lethargy was forgotten as trepidation and distress rolled through her. "It's not like you would have helped them anyway," she muttered.

He offered her a small smile. "Don't be so quick to judge, I'm full of surprises."

She twisted on the cot in order to ease the crick in her neck her position was causing. "You would have helped them?" she demanded.

He flashed all of his white teeth as he winked devilishly. "If I thought it would be fun I would have."

Cassie was baffled by his behavior and cavalier attitude. The Julian she knew was ruthless, monstrous, and a cold hearted killer. This Julian was nothing like that one. This Julian seemed almost cheery and carefree, which seemed completely out of sorts with their environment right now. Cassie shook her head as she tried to rid herself of the confusion swirling through her.

"I don't get you," she muttered.

He dropped onto the bed beneath his window and propped his arm on the sill to study her. "That's the way I like it."

Cassie glowered at him. "You told Isla about my grandmother!"

Another surge of irritation somehow managed to burst past the drug induced lethargy clinging to her. It didn't come raging out of her like it did the night she'd killed Isla, but it coiled through her chest like a serpent unwinding from beneath a rock. Then, whatever they had shot her up with, and whatever they were pumping into her room, took hold of her again.

Cassie blinked as she tried to clear the fog from her mind. She didn't like the idea of going to sleep. If she fell asleep, she wouldn't see them coming for her. If she fell asleep, they *would* get to her again. Cassie shuddered and drew her knees up against her chest in a poor attempt to soothe herself in some way.

"I didn't send Isla after your grandmother." She closed her eyes; she just needed a minute to gather her thoughts. "Hey! Hey!" Cassie's head shot up at the loud banging. Her head whipped around as Julian slapped his hands on the glass one more time. "Stay awake! I'm *talking* to you!"

Cassie managed a small nod as she blearily focused on him. "I'm awake." Her voice sounded thick, groggy, her tongue felt funny, too heavy.

"I did *not* send Isla after your grandmother."

Cassie frowned at him as he touched upon *that* awful subject. "Then how did she know who my grandmother was?" Her words were slurred due to her strange tongue.

Julian's eyes burned into hers. "I may have known about your grandmother, and I may know many other things about *you*, but I can assure you it was never your grandmother I was after."

When Cassie only continued to stare at him questioningly, he continued. "It was *you*."

Her hands dug into her legs in an attempt to keep herself awake. Just what exactly, and how much, did he know about her? "You told Isla about my grandmother though," she grated.

Anger coursed through her when his mouth quirked in amusement. "No princess, it didn't take a rocket scientist to figure out about your grandmother, or you. Even Isla, who had many admirable attributes, but not too much in the way of brains, was able to put two and two together." Cassie's scowl deepened at the mention of Isla's attributes. "I told her to stay away from your grandmother."

"Why would you do that?"

He tilted his head as he studied her. "I didn't plan to poke the bear, not yet anyway."

Cassie blinked at him in stunned surprise. "Excuse me?"

"I wasn't ready to disturb the hornet's nest I sensed inside of you. Isla didn't care about my warnings, or heed them obviously.

She was too bent on trying to get her revenge." His eyes drifted toward the glass behind her. "She paid for that."

"Is that why you tried to keep Devon from getting to me that night, so Isla could get what she deserved? Or me for that matter?" she accused, not at all believing what he was saying to her.

Julian sat back on his heels. She could almost see the wheels turning in his brain as he tried to decide what he was willing to reveal. Finally, he shrugged and leaned forward again. "No, I intervened because I had to be certain. No matter how much I'd advised Isla against it, she did give me the opportunity I needed to observe you."

Cassie moved closer to the window as she strained to hear him better. The fog in her mind seemed to clear as she became riveted upon what he was saying. "Had to be certain of what?"

"Of what you *are*, of course."

Cassie's mouth parted, her hands slipped away from her pants. "What do you mean?"

"When I touched you that first time, I learned you believed you have no powers."

"I *don't* have any powers," she inserted.

Julian's eyes were chips of ice when they met hers. "Then how do you explain a single Hunter being able to take out a vampire who was nearly an Elder?"

Cassie bit on her bottom lip as she recalled the hatred and fury that had filled her the night she'd killed Isla. As much as she'd hated the feeling, and the torment that had accompanied it, she almost wished she could bring that monster out now. *Almost.* It had been awful, and sadistic, and nearly destroyed her. No matter how much she hated their current situation; she hated the creature inside of her more.

"Whatever is inside of me, it's not a power," Cassie broke off as her gaze slid toward the mirror across from her once more. "It's a curse. It's a... it's something awful," she finished on a whisper.

"*They* will tell you it is something awful," Julian hissed. "But they created your race, so they created you."

Cassie swallowed heavily as she shook her head. "I'm confused," she breathed.

Turning, he rested his shoulder against the mirror and dropped his head to the glass. Cassie realized whatever they were pumping into the rooms was having an effect on him too. "When I first met you, I was determined to kill you, not because of what you are but because I aimed to hurt Devon. Though I am very certain your blood would be an amazing treat." Cassie glared at him as he offered her a roguish grin that had probably melted many hearts in his extensive life. Despite herself, Cassie couldn't hold her annoyance with him. She didn't know if it was the drugs, or the bizarre fact she almost liked this strange new Julian. "It was a challenge to get to you, and I love a challenge."

"I see," she murmured.

"I am what I am." He showed no remorse for the things he'd done to her, and her friends, but she'd never expected any from him. It wasn't in his nature to show regret. "But when I touched you and saw what was inside of you," he shrugged. "You are a danger Cassie, to everyone around you, but you are also a force to be reckoned with. I wanted to see how that power could be used, and what it was capable of. I knew you could beat Isla, if you unleashed it..."

"And if I hadn't?"

He shrugged again. "You would have been killed, but I had to see what would happen." She knew she should be annoyed by his nonchalant attitude, but she couldn't find it in herself to be. It was

Julian after all, and although she didn't really mind *this* Julian, he was what he was. "And *Devon* had to see what you were capable of. Though I think he suspected what was inside of you before then."

Cassie yawned again as she rested her head against the glass. She was dimly aware that their heads would have been touching if there hadn't been any glass between them. "Yes, he did. But why would you want him to know about it?"

"Because he *had* to know. If Isla couldn't beat you, and there is a chance *I* may not be able to take you, he had to know if he changed you, like I know he wants to, then there was a good possibility *no* one could beat you if it went wrong. That you could very well destroy us all, including your friends. Although it would have destroyed Devon to watch you become a monster, which would have made me very happy, I couldn't allow such a thing to happen. I enjoy my existence too much for something like that. I don't need you scouring the earth trying to destroy us all."

Cassie managed to shoot him another dirty look, but there was no resentment in his gaze. Instead, there was an odd sense of compassion. Cassie shivered, disarmed and disoriented by this strange new Julian. "I may not become a monster," she retorted.

"No, but there is no way to know, and either way you may still become more powerful than the rest of us."

Cassie fought against closing her eyes again. "These people must realize that," she whispered. "So why wouldn't they just destroy me?"

"I don't know. What they plan on doing with the two of us is not something I care to contemplate. They've left me alone, but now that you're here..."

Cassie lifted her head as his voice trailed off. He was still awake however, his strange eyes distant as he stared at the far wall. "This is going to be awful."

The lazy look he gave her was sympathetic. "I believe so."

Cassie shuddered; she rapidly blinked back the tears burning her eyes. "They'll come for us if we go to sleep, won't they?"

He hesitated, and she could tell he wanted to sugarcoat it, but in the end he didn't. "Yes."

CHAPTER SIXTEEN

"WHERE COULD HE BE?" Devon demanded.

Chris took a hasty step away from him. "Devon, I don't think he's in this area anymore," Annabelle said nervously. "You haven't been able to find him, Chris can't sense him, and Melissa has had no premonitions. We need another plan."

He was such a crazily swinging pendulum of emotions lately that even *he* was surprised he hadn't cracked. It had been three days; she had been missing for *three* days! Three days in which they could have done anything to her.

He shuddered as he battled not to lose his temper again as he had yesterday. He tried not to think about the rampage he'd gone on yesterday, the destruction he'd done to the trees that had been in his way. If he had gotten his hands on something alive, he would have ripped it to shreds whether it had been animal or human.

"What though?" he grated.

Annabelle stared at him helplessly. Liam and Luther had made their way into Vermont, but they weren't having much luck either. He hadn't said it, but Devon knew Liam was concerned the trail was growing cold. "I don't know," she whispered.

Devon nearly bellowed in rage as he slammed his fist into a large oak. The tree shuddered, and its empty branches creaked loudly as it swayed. He could feel the demon in him trying to take over and bury the man. He was greatly afraid he was going to lose the battle, and himself, in the process. He would never be able to find Cassie if he did.

"What do we do?" he asked hopelessly. He had to find her, and he had to do so before he completely lost himself.

"We find another way, maybe there is another one like Julian out there," Melissa said as her gaze warily focused on the oak he had just punched.

"How do we find them?" Chris asked.

"Luther might know," Annabelle replied. "There may be a Hunter out there who has Julian's ability."

"And we're supposed to trust them to help us?" Chris retorted.

"Chris," Melissa cautioned.

Chris shook his head at her as he studied the night surrounding them. An owl hooted in the distance, its mournful sound set Devon's teeth on edge. He paced restlessly away from the tree as he tugged anxiously at his hair. He couldn't take much more of this, his insides felt like something was clawing them to shreds, his skin was on fire, and every muscle of his body was twisted.

There was only one thing, one *person*, who could help to alleviate the agony in him, and he had no idea where she was, or how to find her. He had sent her away to keep her safe, and instead he had put her right in the path of danger. He never should have left her side; he *never* should have let her out of his sight. This was his fault, and Cassie was the one paying for it.

When he found her, *if* he found her, he would never make that mistake again. He looked helplessly back at the rest of them, he needed their help. He couldn't think straight, he needed them to do it for him. "Are you still unable to reach out with your mind?" Annabelle asked him.

At one time he'd been able to brush against her mind with his, but now he was unable to locate her or feel her. "The distance is too great, and I... I am..."

"Too unstable," Annabelle finished when he couldn't.

"Yes," he growled.

She paced amongst the trees as she tried to work things out. She appeared diminutive and sweet, but Annabelle had a spine of steel and a razor-sharp mind. "I think we should join Liam and Luther. We may be able to help them; Melissa might have a premonition. Hopefully," she added. "And Chris may be able to sense something. Maybe if we all join together again we can find her, and if we get close enough to her, you may be able to connect with her again."

Devon remained mute as he stared fixedly at the three of them. Melissa and Annabelle stood proudly, defiantly. Chris looked completely lost and helpless. Devon felt his insides twist more as fresh torment surged through his gut. Fire burned his veins. It wasn't much of a plan, they all knew that, but it was all they had left. He couldn't admit defeat, because if he did it would be over for him and Cassie. He could quite possibly destroy every one of these people, his friends, if he didn't find her. He would definitely find a way to destroy himself, even if it meant staying in the sun for days on end until his body couldn't take it and he finally burned.

"Let's go."

Devon turned and disappeared into the woods as he rapidly ran toward Cassie's house. He didn't wait for the others; he had to burn off some of his excess energy and ire. He raced through the trees, easily dodging the branches and bushes threatening to catch hold of him.

He broke free of the woods and dashed across Cassie's backyard. Pulling out his phone, he hit Luther's number as he slammed into the kitchen. "Anything?" he demanded the minute Luther picked up.

"No," Luther reluctantly admitted.

Devon glanced up as Annabelle came through the back door, and stomped her boots off, as she blew on her hands. Devon's lip curled in a sneer, he hated the pity he felt radiating from her. Turning away, his hand tightened on the phone as he pressed it closer to his ear. "We're coming to join you."

"Excuse me?" Luther asked in surprise.

"We're coming to join you. We're leaving as soon as possible; meet you in Vermont by morning."

Luther was thoughtful for a moment. "All of you?"

"Yes."

Devon heard the rustle of his glasses as Luther slid them off. "We can't leave the town unprotected."

The front door opened and closed, Melissa and Chris appeared in the dining room doorway. "It won't be unprotected, Julian isn't here anymore. I don't know why he moved on, but he has. The Commission won't come here; they already have what they coveted. If other vampires do arrive, they will move on once they realize there are no Hunters here anymore. We're coming up there. *Now*."

"Wait Devon, slow down." Luther said quickly. "Are you sure Julian isn't there?"

"I'm sure," Devon stated.

"The town..."

"Will be fine," Devon interrupted. "This is the only hope we have. We must find her. Are there Hunters out there who possess Julian's ability?"

"I wouldn't know where to start looking," Luther admitted. "The few Hunters who are still accounted for don't have the same ability as Julian. If there are others out there, I don't know where they are."

Devon slammed his hand into the wall with enough force to shake the bracings behind the plastering. "Then this is the only hope we have. I'll call you to find out where you are when we hit the border."

Devon hung up before Luther could say anymore. Rage raced up and down his spine. No one moved for a moment, and then Annabelle strode forward and grasped hold of his arm. "Devon, if this doesn't work we should talk about what will happen."

His gaze landed on his reflection in the window. His eyes were the same murderous red color they'd been ever since Melissa's vision. A color he knew would not vanish until he had Cassie in his arms again. A color he knew meant he was standing on a very thin precipice, one that was about to give way.

"I know what will happen," he told her.

"And what is that?" she asked.

"I'll die, and you will have to help make sure it happens."

Annabelle's sea green eyes swam with tears. He'd never understood how she could forgive him for what he'd done to her, but she had, and she actually *cared* for him. It would have been better if she'd hated him for his cruelty and selfishness. He would only hurt her again if he lost complete control. He touched her hand to offer her some comfort, but he knew it was little.

"It's ok," he assured her. "It's what I will want."

Tears slid down her face as she nodded. "I understand."

Devon slid his arm away from Annabelle and turned on his heel as he left the room.

CHAPTER SEVENTEEN

CASSIE COULDN'T HELP IT; a scream finally ripped from her. The brutality of it tore the inside of her throat apart; the length of it left her breathless and panting for air. She shook with the force of the scream, as she fought against shedding the tears filling her eyes. Sweat poured down her face as she strained to break free, her wrists and shoulders throbbed as she fought against the straps holding her down.

The hours had all blurred into one, she had no concept of time, or days. For all she knew, she had been here only a day, or it could have been a month. She had no thought for time anymore, she barely had thought for consciousness. More often than not, it was the pain that dragged her deep into the realm of unconsciousness until the pain woke her again.

A fresh bolt of electricity caused her body to arch off the table; her feet, wrist, and head restraints were the only things keeping her bound to it. She bit down on her mouth guard as she fought against the urge to scream again. She didn't intend for them to enjoy her torment, but she knew they were enjoying it no matter what. However, her screams would only enhance their pleasure.

She didn't know why they kept pumping her full of electricity, but after a number of jolts they would come back in, take her blood pressure, and pull more blood. She suspected they may be doing the same thing to Julian, but she hadn't seen him since she'd woken up on this table today, yesterday, or whenever it was.

She collapsed upon the table again, and her head lolled to the side. She could feel blood in her mouth from where she'd bit her tongue through the guard, but she couldn't bring herself to care. She watched through half open eyes as they came back into the room. One of them was the cold older man who had been with Joey the first day, the other she didn't know. They didn't speak as they produced more needles.

Cassie groaned she was unable to bear the thought of another needle being shoved into her arm. She held her breath, hating herself for the single tear that slipped down her face as the needle pierced her raw skin. She waited for the tugging feel of her blood being drawn against her will, but it didn't come. Instead, she felt a rush in her arm as something moved through her veins. They brought forth three more syringes and inserted all of their contents into her brutalized veins.

Terror coursed through her. This was new; they had never *injected* her with anything before. She waited breathlessly as she waited to see if they had just decided to put her out of her misery. She wasn't so sure she would mind anymore. Then she thought of Devon and drew his image vividly in her mind. His memory was the only thing keeping her going and remotely sane.

Sometimes she wondered if she was already dead, and this was Hell. But then she would think of Devon, and that small bit of Heaven would prove to her this couldn't be Hell. She was sure nothing in Hell would allow her to feel as good as the thoughts of him did.

"Release her."

Cassie groaned in relief as the agonizing bonds were removed from her. She tried to roll over, tried to stand, but she couldn't move. Hands seized hold of her and roughly lifted her up. Nausea swamped her, for a frightening instant she thought she was going to vomit everywhere. A groan escaped her as they hauled her forward, dragging her when her feet wouldn't move.

Her arm continued to burn as a fire crept through her veins. Her head spun, she tried to regain control of her body but her feet wouldn't cooperate as they simply drug limply behind. If she could regain control, then maybe she could fight them off, but there was no fight in her right now.

She listened as doors opened and closed. Lights bounced roughly off of the stark linoleum beneath her and she blinked against the harsh glare. Nausea rolled through her stomach again, but this time she couldn't hold it back.

Choking, gagging, she heaved the meager contents of her stomach upon the floor. The foul taste of bile made her retch. The men holding her made sounds of revulsion, but they didn't stop as they pulled her through the mess she'd left behind. Another door opened and she was shoved roughly forward. Stumbling, Cassie tripped and sprawled upon the solid ground of her tiny cell. She remained on her knees, unable to move as she wheezed for breath and fought the urge to vomit again. Her body shook, her muscles felt like pretzels, and though the burning in her arm hadn't intensified, it hadn't lessened either.

She tried to push herself to her feet, but her weak and trembling muscles wouldn't allow her to stand. She collapsed on the floor and curled into a ball as she fought against the violent shivers wracking her body. Clamping her teeth together, it took all she had not to scream again as she was hit with bone wrenching spasms. Sweat poured down her body, coated her skin and plastered her clothes to her.

At some point in time unconsciousness claimed her once more. She awoke again, still curled up in a ball, freezing cold and an aching mass. Her cramped muscles screamed in protest as she uncurled herself. She was unable to suppress the moan that escaped her as she crawled forward.

Reaching the bed, she somehow managed to drag herself onto it before passing out once more.

When she awoke again, her body still ached, but every movement wasn't as excruciating as it had been before she passed out. There was a plate of food on the floor by the door. She stared at it, unable to decide if she should eat it, or if she wanted to tempt fate again by moving. Eventually the rumbling in her stomach won out.

Climbing gingerly off the mattress she made her way to the tray, using the wall for support. Creeping away from the wall, she grabbed hold of the tray and cautiously made her way back to the bed. She stared at the darkened mirror of Julian's room. A hollow feeling filled her at the thought of him being gone. Though he would probably still rip her throat out if given the chance, she thought of him as a strange sort of ally now. Both of them were here against their will, and both of them were enduring the same torment. Or at least she assumed Julian was going through the same torment she was.

Turning away, she sat on her bed as she poked through the contents of her tray. There was a bowl of soup, a large piece of French bread, and a tuna fish sandwich. She'd never been a big fan of soup or tuna, but her rumbling stomach didn't care what her taste buds craved. Picking up the sandwich she was about to take a bite when it occurred to her they had probably drugged her food too.

She paused with the sandwich halfway to her mouth. Dropping it back down, she tried to ignore the protesting rumble of her stomach. She couldn't recall the last time she'd had the opportunity to eat. She wanted to refuse the food, but she simply couldn't.

She was starving, and it was essential she have some kind of nutrients, if she was ever going to have a chance of escaping. Biting deep into the sandwich, she ignored the taste of it as she chewed and swallowed quickly. The soup was cold, but tolerable if she used the bread to sop it up first.

Her stomach was still rumbling after she finished, but she felt a little better. When she rose again, she didn't almost fall over. She dropped the tray by the door and turned toward the bathroom. She'd noticed a small shower stall in there the other day, and right now that sounded like a little bit of heaven to her.

The shower head and two knobs came out of the wall. It was set up like a shower on a boat with no curtain, or door; there was simply a drain beneath it. Cassie glanced at the small counter by the sink. There was a travel size bar of soap and shampoo set next to a towel, and a brush on the other side. There was also no mirror above the sink.

Cassie stripped out of her soiled clothes and turned the shower on as hot as she could stand it. The heat and pounding spray helped to soothe some of the tension in her knotted muscles. The water was turning cold before she abandoned it. Her body felt much better; her muscles were looser and not as twisted. Though she wasn't back to normal, she could now at least move without wincing with every step.

Beneath the towel she found a set of blue medical scrubs. She was loath to put anything on they'd given her. Glancing back at her soiled and stinking clothes she realized she couldn't put them back on. They reeked of vomit, BO, and sweat. Wrinkling her nose at them, she grabbed hold of the scrubs and quickly slipped them on.

She found a toothbrush and a small tube of toothpaste; at least her teeth wouldn't rot out while she was here. She brushed for a while, eager to get the lingering taste of bile and fish out of her mouth. She worked the tangles out of her hair, wishing they'd thought to leave her conditioner, but knowing she'd already received more than she could have hoped for. They had probably only given her these things because they had also grown tired of the stench of her.

Feeling almost human again, she made her way out of the bathroom and turned the switch off. She was surprised, and relieved, to find the light in Julian's room was on. She hurried toward her bed and knelt upon it as she eagerly peered into his room. By the door was a small bag of blood that made her feel somewhat ill again.

Glancing down, she found Julian lying upon his bed with his arm draped over his eyes. He was also freshly showered with a pair of blue scrubs on. Though he looked clean, and somewhat refreshed, there were tense lines around his mouth and his eyes were squinted shut. It was obvious he was battling the remnants of torture also.

Julian moved his arm and peered up at her with one eye. "You weren't here earlier," she said.

"No, I wasn't. You're looking better than yesterday."

Cassie started in surprise. "I was here yesterday?" she croaked.

Amusement flickered across his features. "You were here, but you were barely functioning."

Cassie slumped down on her bed. She didn't even remember

being in this room yesterday, how bad had she been? What had they done to her that could possibly be worse than the unending volts of electricity she'd received today? "What did they do to me?" she whispered.

Julian was silent and then his head appeared over top of the window. "I don't know Princess, but it wasn't pretty. You were a slobbering, blubbering mess."

Cassie's eyes narrowed at his assessment of her condition. "Well, I don't remember it!" she retorted.

He grinned at her and the lines on his face eased a little. "Don't get so defensive; I'm just stating a truth."

Cassie looked at the door behind her and drew her knees up against her chest. She rested her chin on her knees as dread and horror filtered through her. "How long have I been in here?"

"I don't know," he admitted reluctantly. "Just as I don't know how long *I've* been here."

She turned her attention back to him. "What have they been doing to you?"

He frowned at her and shook back his still damp hair. "The same as they've probably been doing to you."

"I don't remember a lot of it," she admitted reluctantly.

"You're lucky then."

Cassie shuddered as she began to rock slightly back and forth. "If you call this lucky."

He issued a harsh bark of laughter. "No, I call this a bunch of bored men who have too much time on their hands, and some severe mommy and daddy issues. I call this insanity."

Cassie couldn't help but smile at him as she shook her head. "You're right. Aren't you going to eat?" she inquired as she nodded toward the bag by the door.

"No, I don't trust them not to have drugged it."

"Neither do I, but you have to keep up your strength.

Besides, I ate the food and I'm still standing. If they are going to drug us all they have to do is pump it into our rooms. Eat Julian."

He hesitated before shaking his head. "Maybe later." Cassie sat back on the bed and rested her head against the glass. "You ok princess?"

"No, are you?"

He settled in next to her. "Better than before, apparently they've decided to leave us alone for a while."

Cassie snorted softly. "Probably so they can play with the copious amounts of blood they drained from me."

"Hmm," he muttered.

"Did they take blood from you?"

"Yes."

Cassie's hands fisted on her legs, a sting in her arm drew her attention back to it. Though it had stopped burning, it still felt strange and tingly. Releasing her legs, she pushed back the sleeve of her scrubs. Her arm was puckered and bruised with needle marks, but one mark was dark blue with streaks of purple winding out to emphasize her veins. She could see whatever they had put into her working its way through her bloodstream.

Her breath exploded from her as a strangled cry escaped. Julian's head turned toward her, but she couldn't stop the strange, animalistic noises escaping her. Bolting upright in bed, she clawed at her arm as she tried to rip the purple from it. When that didn't work, she began to squeeze it as she tried to push the poison, or whatever it was, back out of her body.

"Cassie! Cassie!"

She was dimly aware of Julian's shouts as she pushed harder and harder. Her arm began to bleed as she clawed at it. Cassie bolted off the bed and scrambled to get away. But there was no escape; she couldn't escape her own skin. She tripped over her own feet and fell to the floor. Her knees screamed in protest, but she barely felt it over the mind numbing revulsion consuming her.

The discoloration seemed to have stopped spreading but it wasn't receding from her veins. She was unaware of the tears spilling down her face until they plopped onto her arm to mix with her blood. The mewls and squeals coming from her weren't human, but the noises of a frightened, cornered animal, which was exactly what she felt like.

"Cassandra!" The loud bangs reverberating through the room finally pierced her panic stricken mind. "*Cassandra*!"

She choked back the sobs clogging her throat. The shaking racking through her left her muscles throbbing and her bones full of pain once more. She leaned over her arm as she clung to it and closed her eyes against the ugly discoloration.

"Cassie," Julian's voice was tinged with apprehension. "Cassie *look* at me."

She took a shuddery breath as she tried to regain her rapidly unraveling composure. Though she realized she was on the verge of losing her sanity, she couldn't bring herself to care. "Cassandra, look at me!" he ordered.

Ever so slowly, she lifted her head and focused her attention upon him. He was staring back at her with his hands resting above his head on the glass. His shoulders sagged in relief as she focused upon him. Tears continued to slide down her face.

"Come here," he commanded.

Closing her eyes, Cassie took a deep breath as she tried to gather her shaking muscles. She continued to cling to her arm as she stumbled to her feet and held it away from her as if it were a poisonous snake. Which at this point, to her, it was.

"Let me see," he ordered roughly when she was close enough.

Cassie bit her bottom lip, she was unable to look again as she held her arm out to him. She watched his face and saw his pupils dilate at the sight of her blood. Fangs extended briefly before he shook his head to clear away his hunger for her blood. "What does it feel like?" he demanded.

Cassie shuddered. "It burned when they put it in," she whispered, unable to keep the tremor from her voice.

His eyes rapidly scanned her face. "And how do you feel now?"

"I don't know. Freaked out, scared."

"How do you feel *physically*?"

His voice was harsher than it had been; his eyes more intense. Cassie stared at him, surprised by his forcefulness. "Like crap, but I suppose that's what happens when you've been blasted with electricity for hours on end." He relaxed somewhat, but she could sense a current of tension running through him. "Do you know what caused this?"

His eyes were distant as they met hers. "No."

Cassie couldn't shake the unsettling feeling he was lying to her. Taking a deep breath, she sat back on the bed and dropped her arm to her side. She refused to look at it again, terrified by what she might see there. "Did they give you anything like this?"

He tilted his head to the side. "No, they didn't give me anything like that."

"But they took your blood too?" she inquired.

He nodded as he ran his hand through his platinum hair. "Yes, they did."

Cassie folded her hands in her lap, careful not to look at her arm again as she curled up on the bed once more. "I think I'm going to lose my mind," she admitted.

"You can't do that."

"And why not?"

"Cause I can't be stuck in this shithole by myself."

She chuckled, but a single tear slid down her face as she rested her head on the glass again. "If it weren't for this glass you would rip out my throat."

He laughed. "I'm not so sure I could take you princess, and like I said before, I do enjoy my existence."

"But you would give it a try?"

His eyebrow cocked in amusement. "I do love a challenge, but no, probably not."

She turned her head to look at him, surprised to find him curled up next to her again, his head resting above hers, and his shoulders pressed against the glass by hers. Once again she was struck with the realization that if the glass wasn't between them, they would be touching. She found the thought didn't make her stomach turn as much as it once had.

He was not such a bad guy, for a cold blooded killer, she amended.

"Then why did you come after me the night of the homecoming dance? You'd touched me before that night, you'd almost killed me before then.

His grin broadened as his eyes twinkled. "Yeah, that was a good night," he replied wistfully. Cassie shot him a fierce look, his smile only grew. "Oh, come on Princess, we had fun that night."

"Yeah it was a blast," she muttered.

"It was," he agreed as he remembered the night with a lot more fondness than she did. Then again, he hadn't almost bled to death. "I didn't get much of an impression off of you the first time we met. If you do recall, I barely got my hands on you."

"Just enough to slit my throat open, and don't tell me that was fun," she charged.

"Not as much fun as our fight at your homecoming dance. That was a blast." He only grinned at her as she scowled at him. "That was when I really discovered what you were capable of, and if you do recall, I tended to stay away afterward."

"Yes, you did," she whispered. "Do you think Devon is close to finding us?"

Julian snorted weakly. "He's not looking for *me,* Princess, at least not here anyway. But no, I don't believe so."

"Are you always so pessimistic?" she inquired.

"Just pragmatic. *We* don't know where we are, how could he possibly find us?" He shook his head as his eyes closed briefly. "Would be a miracle."

Cassie tried not to let her doubt and fear swamp her. "I believe in miracles."

"No, you believe in Devon."

Cassie looked at him in surprise. "Excuse me?"

"You don't believe in miracles, you *believe* in *Devon.*"

She contemplated his words. She did believe in Devon, she did have faith he would find her. "Yes, yes I do. He *will* find us. He won't give up until he does."

"No, he won't." He agreed with her, but she could tell Julian didn't put much faith in her words. "But the likelihood of him finding us is small; we have to come up with a plan. It's essential we get *ourselves* out of this."

"How?" she whispered as her gaze flitted toward the dark mirror opposite her. She was frightened they were listening, that though she couldn't see them, they could still hear her.

"You." Cassie no longer cared if they were listening as she turned back to him. "When I touched you Cassie, it was a shock of power unlike any I've ever felt before. If we're going to get out of this, you are going to have to find that power..."

"I can't control it, and they have me drugged," she interrupted.

"You can break through it, I *know* you can."

Cassie met his fevered gaze. "You don't want me to"

"Yes, I do. We *need* to get out of here Princess, before they kill us, or turn us into something...."

Cassie frowned as his voice trailed off, her heart turned over at his words. "Turn us into something?"

His eyes were remorseless as they met hers briefly before nodding toward her arm. "What do you think they gave you?"

She refused to look at her arm again; she would vomit if she did. "I don't know. I don't *want* to know." The band of white in his eyes momentarily flashed red. "Should I be worried, Julian?"

He shook his head as his eyes became normal again. "No Princess, you're fine, but they will give you more. Maybe even something else. We can't stay here and be their guinea pigs." Cassie bowed her head to her knees. "I know you believe in Devon, but you have to accept that he may not be able to find us. Between the two of us, we *can* get out of here."

"Or I could turn on you," she replied miserably.

A muscle ticked in his cheek. "I can take care of myself, Princess."

"Yeah, that's why you're here," she retorted, tired of being called Princess.

His eyebrows lifted sharply before he burst into loud laughter. Cassie's mouth parted in surprise, his laugh was actually pleasant. It was warm, and easy, and had a surprising amount of humor in it. She found herself watching him in fascination, unable to stop herself from smiling along with him.

"Very true, but let's not focus on me in this; let's focus on getting our asses out of here."

Cassie continued to grin at him. "You know, you're not so bad when you're in here, and you have a nice laugh."

He chuckled as he rested his forehead on the glass and stared down at her. "I don't remember the last time I laughed," he admitted. "And you had better be careful, it almost sounds like you're flirting with me, Princess."

Her mouth parted in surprise, and then a burst of laughter escaped her. "Hardly," she retorted.

"Come on, admit it, you find me a little appealing."

Cassie shook her head at him, unable to stop herself from laughing again. She did find him a little appealing and was actually beginning to like him a little. Even if she didn't trust him not to drain her dry the second he got the chance. "Well, you're not as repulsive as these people at least."

He flashed all of his perfect white teeth. "That's good to know, at least I'm moving up on your list."

"You are."

She rested her head against the glass again. She wished Devon was with her, to comfort her, to take her away from here. Closing her eyes, she pictured his face in vivid detail. She could clearly recall the smell of him, the feel of him. She could almost taste him again, and feel his lips against hers. For a brief moment it was as if he were there, as if she could actually touch him.

Then it was gone, and she was left alone in her small cell with no one to comfort or touch her. Cassie fought back the tears burning her eyes. "Don't fall apart on me, you're tougher than that."

Cassie fought to suppress the sobs threatening to shake her. Tears rolled down her face as her breath hitched out of her. "Hey," Julian said harshly. "Look at me."

She turned toward him and blinked rapidly against the tears

streaming down her face. His hand was pressed against the glass, his face intense. "Put your hand on mine."

She stared blankly at him before lifting her hand and pressing it to the glass. Though they weren't touching, the gesture still helped to sooth the ragged desolation inside of her. She missed being touched with kindness, missed the simple beauty of knowing she had her friends, and Devon, to rely on. She missed Chris, if he was still alive, but that was something she couldn't allow herself to think about, otherwise she would lose complete control of her emotions, and Melissa and Luther. She missed their comfort, support, and unwavering love. She had none of that here. She had *nothing* here.

Except for Julian.

His vivid eyes glowed with a strange sort of luminosity. "Now listen to me. We *are* going to get through this. We *are* going to get out of here, but you have got to keep it together. If you break down in here, they win. You don't want that, do you?" Cassie shook her head. "Good, so stay calm and we will get through this."

Cassie swallowed heavily. "Yes."

"All right then. Why don't you tell me a little about yourself?"

She frowned at him as she settled back on her bed; it seemed like such an odd request coming from him. She kept her hand pressed against his on the glass, she was unable to break the small connection to someone else it gave her. "I thought you knew it all already," she murmured. "You have touched me, and you have given me a good beat down before."

He grinned at her. "You gave as well as you got," he reminded her. "I know a lot about you, but I'd rather hear it coming from you."

She studied him as she tried to assimilate this man with the monster she'd known, with the killer who had hunted her town, and killed so many innocents. Confusion twisted through her as she shook her head. Where was the monster that had tried to destroy her? This person was completely different, this person was someone she didn't know, but was beginning to trust and like.

Cassie was shaken by the odd realization, her hand tightened on the glass as she stared into his beautiful, compassionate eyes. She was fascinated by him, captivated by this stranger who was becoming her friend. Julian was the only person she had to count on right now, and she wouldn't survive this without him.

"What would you like to know?" she asked.

He grinned at her. "Why don't you tell me about your tree house?"

He leaned against the glass with his hand still pressed against hers. She could almost feel the warmth of his hand against hers, the comfort of his touch. Leisurely, fondly, she told him about the tree house she and Chris had spent weeks building when they were ten years old. Only to have it fall apart on them a day after they finished it.

CHAPTER EIGHTEEN

It was the talks that got her through the next few days. Every night she would curl up on her bed, place her hand against the glass and talk with Julian. She told him stories of her childhood, stories he probably already knew, but patiently listened to anyway. They would talk until the drugs kicked in and she drifted into a nightmare filled sleep that was nearly impossible to wake from. They would talk until her throat was raw, and she was sure he was sick of listening to her. The more she talked, and the more he listened, the closer she began to feel to him. The closer they *became* to each other.

The men came for her every day, and although she didn't have to endure more electrical jolts, they came up with other forms of torture. At one point she was locked into a windowless room with a set of strobe lights. It had been a torment that had been brutal against her sensitive eyes. She'd left the room with a massive headache, and had been unable to see for a good hour afterward.

She tried to remain mute through the tortures, tried to hold

Devon's image close to her in order to get through each new thing they came up with for her. But most of the time they broke her. She would end up screaming, and in the room with the lights, they had brought her to tears. It was a fact she was ashamed of, and one she didn't share with Julian. She couldn't bring herself to admit to him she was weaker than she'd *ever* thought she was.

They gave her three more of the same shots; each one had the same effect on her. The strange discoloration would take hold, but by morning it would be gone. She didn't have another freak out, but she wasn't sure she could take much more of it. She held out hope Devon would rescue her, but it was getting tougher to keep her spirits up.

Julian didn't give up hope. His spirits didn't diminish. He kept her sane when it was becoming increasingly difficult to keep her sanity. He was determined they would escape, determined *she* would be the one to get them out. The only problem was he couldn't think of how she was going to do it. He only knew she *would*.

"Cassie."

"Hmm?" Every muscle in her body screamed in protest as she met Julian's inquisitive gaze.

"Are you ok?"

She nodded as she rubbed the bridge of her nose tiredly. Today they had locked her within a dark room with no windows. She'd spent hours curled up in a corner, wondering if they would come back for her, or if this was where they were going to leave her until she died. She'd tried to picture Devon as she huddled in the corner, frightened and alone, trying not to shatter, but it was becoming more difficult to draw upon his image, to remember all of the details in this hideous place.

They had come back for her though. They had given her

another shot, and they had deposited her in her room once more, where Julian had been waiting for her. She had no idea what they were looking for with all of these tests and tortures, no idea what they were trying to do to her, or what they aimed to prove. She only knew it couldn't be good.

She also wondered how much longer they were going to keep them both alive. Once they were done with their tests, and knew whatever it was they were trying to know, she would be of no use to them, and neither would Julian. Cassie shuddered to think they might destroy him before her and leaving her completely alone.

She knew she would break completely if she was left alone. Her sanity would shred, leaving her a shell of the person she had once been. She was beginning to think that was what they truly wanted from her after all. If they were just trying to turn her into a huddled mess, unable to think or act coherently anymore.

"I'm fine," she whispered.

"Why don't you tell me about when you used to ride," he suggested.

Cassie thought back to her early years, when she'd been obsessed with horses, and riding. She'd taken lessons nearly every day, preferring to be on a horse than solid ground. They were the happiest times of her life, but she'd given up riding when Luther had arrived and informed her of her Hunter legacy.

She hadn't thought about riding in years, had almost completely forgotten about it. It seemed like a life time ago now. She had been a completely different person then. *That* Cassie had been hopeful and bright and full of life. *This* Cassie was beaten, nearly broken, and barely clinging to her sanity.

She didn't like to recall that time of her life, or that Cassie. It wasn't comforting to her right now.

"No, I don't want to talk about that, not tonight. Let's talk about you tonight."

Julian looked at her in surprise, but he seemed to sense her morose thoughts. "What would you like to know?"

There was a lot she would like to know about him and his life. But she didn't want to hear about Devon. She didn't think she'd be able to tolerate thoughts of Devon right now, not after today anyway. "How did you become a vampire?" she inquired.

His eyes were shadowed and sunken as they met hers. "I fell in love with the wrong woman," he admitted.

Cassie couldn't believe it, Julian, in love? It seemed impossible, and yet...

She had gotten to know him well since they'd been locked in here. Yes, he was a murderer and he could be vicious and cruel at times, but there was a good man underneath it all. One she'd never expected to find. One she'd never imagined could exist, and one she'd actually come to care for and trust.

"Who was she?" Cassie prompted, afraid he wasn't going to continue.

"She was everything," he whispered. "Smart, sophisticated, and so very beautiful." There was a keen appreciation in his gaze that rattled her. "Almost as beautiful as you."

Cassie's mouth dropped. Julian thought *she* was beautiful? She found herself discomfited by his words, but she was more discomfited that the knowledge caused a strange thrill to run through her. Cassie turned away from him as she tried to ignore the strange turning in her stomach. What was the *matter* with her? Was this some sort of strange dream world her shattered mind had created?

"What was her name?" she asked as she tried to divert herself from her troubling thoughts and feelings.

"Victoria. Her name was Victoria and there wasn't anything I wouldn't do for her, including give up my life, my humanity."

"You can get your humanity back."

He snorted softly. "It's a little too late for that."

She shook her head and swallowed heavily as she met his intense stare once more. "No it's not, Devon changed."

"And you would like it if I was more like Devon?"

There was a taut tone to his voice that told her he wasn't pleased by the notion. "No," she told him. "I like you just the way you are, but you have the choice to take your humanity back if you want it."

His nostrils flared as his eyes perused her. "I suppose you're right," he said tersely. "I could make that choice *if* I wanted to."

"But you don't?"

He shrugged. "I never had a reason to, before."

Cassie itched to relieve the anguish and tension she felt radiating from him. Before what? She wondered, but decided against pursuing that line of questioning. She wasn't sure she would like the answer. Or, if she was truly honest with herself, she was frightened she may like the answer too much. "What happened with Victoria?" she inquired to change the topic.

He shrugged negligently. "I fell in love, she changed me, and I became a monster. I think she did so mainly so she could have a puppet to play with and use. She never loved me, and though she enjoyed toying with my emotions, she quickly became bored with me. I woke up one day and she was gone."

Cassie's heart ached for the melancholy and loss she sensed beneath his cavalier tone. "I'm sorry."

He shrugged again. "It's all good; I got over that bitch years ago. Truth be told, I didn't think our kind was capable of love, until you and Devon. When I touched him and felt the vast amount of love he has for you, it fascinated me."

Cassie guiltily glanced away. Devon did love her, whole heartedly. He was probably nearly crazed with his desperation to find her, and she was sitting here, experiencing odd feelings for one of Devon's greatest enemies, one of *her* greatest enemies.

Except he wasn't her enemy anymore, and at one time he'd been Devon's best friend. Julian had become her only sense of comfort, the only thing keeping her alive. In a strange way he had become one of her closest friends. They shared a common bond no one else would understand. They were linked together by this awful experience, and they were the only reason the other was still alive. She'd come closer to losing her mind than he had, but she knew he was just barely clinging to his sanity and composure also.

"I planned to destroy that love."

She looked back at him. "Why?" she demanded.

He shrugged. "Why should Devon get the happy ending I'd been denied?"

Cassie's mouth parted. "And how do you feel now?"

Amusement curved his full mouth making him appear younger and more approachable. "Now I don't."

"Why not?"

He shrugged absently as he dropped his head to the glass. "Because it would upset *you* if I destroyed him."

The breath froze in her lungs, her heart pumped loudly in her chest. Confusion swirled through her as she tried to puzzle out his words, and how she felt about them. "Julian..."

Her words faded away as he turned back to her, and those ice eyes burned into hers. "I know how you feel about him, Princess. I've touched you, and I know the depth of your love for him, the purity of it. I expect nothing from you, and I won't hurt you. Ever."

Tears filled her eyes and slipped down her cheeks. She was

confused by her strange new feelings for him, but she knew he was *not* confused. It was apparent he cared for her deeply, that he may be in love with her. She ached for him, ached for the feelings he had; feelings she couldn't return. Not in the way he desired her to at least. "I'm sorry," she whispered.

"Don't be. This is not a bad thing. I think it's a good thing. You've made me different and I thank you for it. Please don't cry, Princess."

Cassie wiped the tears from her eyes and bit on her bottom lip as she tried to stifle the flow. She couldn't bring herself to look at him again, couldn't stop the swirling confusion rolling through her. He was right, what she felt for Devon was true and so unbelievably good and real. She didn't want Julian to be hurt because of it though. "What happened to Victoria?" she asked.

"She was killed during what you call The Slaughter." Cassie looked at him in surprise. "What, you thought it was only *your* kind who was killed?"

"Yes," Cassie admitted.

He shook his head. "Nope, your kind did put up a fight against us; they took a few of us with them. One of which was Victoria."

She'd never thought about it, hadn't realized it had happened. "I'm sorry for your loss," she told him.

"Don't be, I hadn't seen her in over a hundred years by that point."

Cassie stifled a yawn as whatever they were pumping into her room started to take hold. "We have to get out of here."

"Yes, we do."

Instinctively, she rested her hand against the glass. She sighed in relief as he pressed his large palm against hers. She'd feared he would shut her out, that her inability to return his feelings would turn him against her. "We *will* get out."

"Not counting on Devon to rescue you anymore?"

She had no doubt Devon was tearing the earth apart in search of her, but it was unreasonable of her to expect him to find her. She'd been here for so long, if he was able to find her, he would have by now. "He won't stop until he finds me, but it may not be in time."

"My thoughts exactly, Princess."

She rolled her eyes as she shot him a cross look. "Stop calling me Princess," she grumbled. He grinned back at her. "Didn't you believe in Annabelle and Liam's love?"

He frowned before shaking his head. "I didn't know much about Annabelle and Liam. Devon kept me away from her, she was his own private project, and I let him have her because I thought it would be fun to watch the show. I never thought what happened between them would happen and that Devon could change. At the time I would have interfered if I'd known what was coming."

"But not now?"

His amazing eyes darkened to an almost sea shade of blue. "No. No matter how much I resent Devon for turning against his own kind, his very nature, and me, I am glad he brought you into our lives."

Cassie's fatigue was forgotten in the face of his words. Her heart thumped loudly, her breath was labored as she tried to think of some way to comfort him, some way to sort through the tumult of emotions tearing through her. The vulnerable expression on his face caused tears to bloom in her eyes once more.

"Julian..."

His blond hair fell across his forehead as he offered a tremulous smile. "It's ok Princess, I understand."

She was glad he understood, because she didn't anymore. She dropped her head to the window and found comfort when he rested his head against hers once more. She loved Devon, she knew that, but the idea of causing Julian pain was tearing her to shreds inside. He was her savior, her friend, and she was growing to love and rely on him more and more with every passing moment.

CHAPTER NINETEEN

"WHERE ARE WE?" Chris inquired as he roused from the backseat.

Devon glanced down at the GPS. "Cedarville."

"And where is Cedarville?"

"Upstate New York."

Chris studied the dark woods surrounding them. Moonlight filtered over the skeletal trees and cast shadows across the snow covered hills and mountains. They had been steadily rising in elevation for the past twenty minutes. "So we're in the boonies," Chris muttered.

"Yeah," Devon confirmed as he glanced toward the woods at his side. He hadn't seen Annabelle and Liam in a while, but he knew they were out there somewhere, keeping pace with the slow moving vehicle. Liam was hunting for any animal that may have seen something, and still remembered it. They had been searching New York for over a day now, and Devon was struggling not to give up hope they would find her, but since crossing the border yesterday they'd found no new leads.

His hands gripped the steering wheel as he fought not to rip it free. "Have you heard from them?" Chris asked as he climbed over the middle and slid into the passenger seat. Melissa and Luther were still sleeping in the far back of the Escalade.

"No."

Chris's gaze focused on the dark forest as his forehead furrowed. Devon could tell he was trying to pick up Cassie's presence, and having no luck at it. "Maybe the trail ends here because she's somewhere near here," Chris stated after a few moments.

Devon wished it was that simple, but he didn't believe so. Pulling out his phone, he checked the screen but there were no new messages. He slid it back into his pocket before he shattered it. "Pull over, Devon."

His head snapped toward Chris. "You sense something?"

Chris shook his head. "I have to piss."

"Oh."

Devon pulled over to the side of the road for him. He waited impatiently, his fingers tapping against the steering wheel as Chris disappeared into the night. Devon frowned as he studied the oddly hushed woods. It was too calm out there. Chris appeared by the passenger door again.

"Something's not right in this town," Chris stated. Devon nodded his agreement as he continued to study the forest. "We actually might be in the right area."

Devon tried not to let his expectation's rise, tried not to let his heart soar at the thought, but he couldn't stop the spurt of excitement that shot through him. He turned his attention to the night as he listened for any new sound. "This quiet usually means vampires," he said. "Get back in the car Chris."

"Wait, what?"

"Get in the car!" Devon ordered briskly. He flung his door

open and stepped swiftly into the chilly night. He searched the wood for anything out there, but he could only sense Annabelle and Liam moving steadily closer to the vehicle.

The back window opened and Melissa stuck her head out. "What's going on?"

Devon shook his head as he walked to the back of the SUV. He shot Chris a dark look as he appeared on the other end of the vehicle. "I told you to get inside," he growled.

Chris shook his head and chose to ignore him. "I don't sense anything out there," Chris told him. "Absolutely nothing."

Liam and Annabelle appeared at the edge of the woods and rapidly moved forward. Annabelle's gaze darted constantly over her surroundings while Liam's gaze was focused behind them. "What is this place?" Annabelle inquired.

"Cedarville," Chris answered.

Devon glowered at him. "This place is strange. There's something off about it," Annabelle whispered.

"I don't sense any other vampires though," Liam mumbled. "And for the past two miles there have been very few animals. None of them could help us."

Devon's chest clenched at the idea they'd run out of leads. He couldn't concentrate on that thought; he would crack if he did. There was something off about this place, something not right at all, and he had to stay focused on that. "We should go into town."

"For what?" Chris asked in surprise.

"Because we need to find out what is going on here."

"But what about Cassie..." Chris's voice trailed off as his eyes flitted to the forest. "You think she's here?"

Devon managed a brief nod. He didn't know what to think, but this place was strange, and it was where their trail ended. It was the only hope they had. The only hope *he* had. "Are you going to ride with us, or stick to the woods?" Devon asked Annabelle and Liam.

"I'd like to stay in the woods, see if I can find something," Liam answered. "There has to be some more wildlife out there, somewhere."

Devon nodded as he hurried toward the front of the vehicle. He was eager to get into town and see what it had to offer, and what secrets it was hiding. "What's going on?" Luther inquired the second they were back inside.

"There's something peculiar about this place, we're going to go into town, maybe find some answers," Devon told him.

He pulled back onto the road and hit the gas pedal hard in his eagerness to find the center of town. He glanced at the GPS. A hotel had popped up on the screen about five miles away. A gas station was closer, but there were no other landmarks show-ing. "Small town," Chris muttered.

"Do you think there are answers here?" Melissa asked.

"There is something here," Chris answered. "And a whole lot of nothing."

"I don't understand," Melissa replied.

"There's nothing out there. No wildlife, no people, just *nothing*."

Melissa grasped hold of the back of Devon's seat and leaned forward. "Are you saying this is some kind of strange ghost town?"

"I don't know what it is, but it's not normal."

"Do you think Cassie is here somewhere?"

"I don't know what to think," Devon answered when Chris remained silent. "I do know I have never been in a place like this."

He turned his blinker on, but ended up driving past the gas station as none of the lights were on. "It *is* two o'clock in the morning," Luther reminded him. "We'll be lucky if we can get a room at the motel."

"Hmm," Devon agreed.

"This place is creepy," Melissa muttered as she sat back in her seat. "I keep waiting for zombie's or hill people to come out and attack us."

Devon wasn't going to say he agreed with her, but he couldn't shake the thought of such a thing either. They pulled up to the motel, there were four cars in the parking lot, but the place had a deserted air about it. Devon's senses were on high alert as he stepped from the vehicle.

He didn't hear people moving around inside the building or hear the faint beat of human hearts. He couldn't hear them rustling around in their sleep, breathing, or snoring. "It's so quiet," Melissa breathed.

"There's no one in there," Devon told them.

Melissa and Chris glanced at him, but Luther had retreated back to the SUV in search of something. "Are you certain?" Chris inquired.

"Yes."

"But the cars," Melissa argued.

"This place is empty."

"According to this map Cedarville is twenty-two square miles with a population of two hundred and fifty people. This is the only motel on the GPS and it appears Cedarville mainly consists of dairy farms," Luther announced as he returned from the SUV with a map book in his hands. "Though they do have a small center of town, and a school."

"We should go in there and see if there are any clues about what happened to these people," Devon told them.

"Wait," Chris said and grabbed hold of his arm. "What if

you're wrong? What if there are people still in there? We can't just go barging in."

Devon stared at him for a moment before pulling his arm free. "There is no one left in there, and if there was, I would just change their memories." Chris was still hesitant, his eyes doubtful as he gazed back at the motel. "We're wasting time, we have to go."

Devon didn't wait for them as he quickly made his way across the parking lot. Snow crunched under his feet, and the wind whipped around him. He shoved his hands into the pockets of his jacket, but he barely noted the chill. He needed answers, and he needed them now. Stepping onto the sidewalk running down the front of the building, he went for the first room he came across.

Grasping hold of the doorknob, he pulled down forcefully and slammed it open. "Devon!" Melissa hissed.

He didn't give her a second thought as he shoved the door open further and flipped on the light switch. The room was in neat order and the bed made. There was no lingering scent of human within, no bags marking this as one of the rooms that had been occupied. He didn't bother to close the door before moving hastily onto the next one.

He went quickly through the next few rooms and found all of them as deserted as the first. Finally he came across a room that had been occupied recently. He stepped into the room, glad to be out of the cold air and howling wind. The comforter on the bed had been turned down, a suitcase sat on a chair beside the bed with its top open to reveal men's clothing.

An old Married with Children episode was running on the TV. Devon barely glanced at it as his attention was riveted on the empty room. There was no sign of a scuffle, but the room was empty and the person seemed to have vanished.

He left the room and hurried down the walkway. He rapidly went through the rest of the rooms, but there were no answers to be found in any of them either. Another man appeared to have been staying in one of them, and a couple in the other. He arrived at the manager's office, frustration and anger boiled through him as he grabbed hold of the knob.

"Wait," Melissa whispered as she seized hold of his arm.

He was surprised by the pallor of her skin, the firm set of her full lips. There was a haunted look about her black eyes that made his blood run cold. The last time he'd seen that look on her face he'd lost the only person he'd ever truly cared about.

"Cassie?" he breathed.

She shuddered as she took an unsteady breath and broke free of the premonition. "No," she moaned as she took a small step back. "No. That room, it's awful, just awful."

Luther took hold of her shoulders as she quickly turned away. His eyes were haunted as they briefly met Devon's. Bracing for whatever it was Melissa had seen, Devon turned the handle and was surprised to find it unlocked. He shoved the door open. The beast in him reared to turbulent life, and hunger sprang forth as the sweet scent of blood assailed him.

He closed his eyes against the demon clamoring at his insides. His fangs had elongated at the smell and bit into his lower lip. "Are you ok?" Chris inquired tremulously.

Fisting his hands, Devon managed a small nod. It still took him a few minutes to regain complete control though. He ground his teeth together as he flipped the switch. Disgust and excitement rolled through him in equal measures when he took in the room. He hated the part of himself becoming excited by the carnage of the room, but he couldn't stop it. He'd caused this, and worse, in his lengthy life.

"My God," Chris breathed.

"This has nothing to do with God," Devon replied crisply.

He cautiously moved into the room, and stepped over the broken bits of chair littering the floor. The customary hotel painting of a serene landscape hung on the wall, completely out of place amidst all of the destruction and mayhem. Papers were scattered about; they mixed with the blood splattered everywhere. A large smear of blood covered the back wall, and it seemed the victim had been lifted to the ceiling and then pulled back down to the floor.

Devon stepped around the desk and the feet of the victim came into view. He shuddered, his hands fisted harder as he fought against the bloodlust threatening to consume him. He braced himself for the mayhem as he stepped completely around the desk.

The manager's body was sprawled across the floor; his arms and legs were twisted at the unnatural angle of a man who'd had his back broken. His neck was turned to the side; his unseeing brown eyes focused upon the ceiling. His stomach was torn open, his intestines were gone, and his throat had been nearly ripped out.

Devon's skin turned to ice as he took in the room. There wasn't enough blood here for the savage gashes. It hadn't been a human attacker who had done this, but it hadn't been a vampire either. No vampire would eat the intestines.

"We have to go!" he barked.

"What is it?" Luther demanded.

Devon's gaze went to the door that most likely led into the manager's apartment. He didn't sense another presence back there, but he wasn't so sure he would. "Chris?" he inquired.

Chris glanced at him and then rapidly surveyed the room before shaking his head. "I don't sense anyone else," he said.

Devon nodded, but it didn't soothe the tension knotting his stomach. "Come on, we must get out of here."

"What's the matter?" Luther asked.

"Halfling," Devon answered as he turned away from the body.

"Wait! What?" Chris sputtered. "One of those monster things? One of those things you were scared *Cassie* might become?"

"Yes."

Luther paled as he took a step back. Devon pushed them out the door. Melissa was still huddled outside, her cheeks red from the cold, and her eyes shadowed and haunted. Devon studied the dark night, his senses on hyper alert as he watched for any sign of movement. "Come on, we can't stay here."

He hurried them forward, practically shoving Chris toward the car. Throwing open the driver's side door, he slid in, and waited until everyone was settled before he locked the doors and pulled out his cell phone and dialed Annabelle's number. "Where are you guys?" he demanded when she picked up.

"Not far from you," she replied.

"You need to get here."

"What's wrong?" she inquired nervously.

"You have to get here and be careful," Devon told her.

"We'll be there soon."

Devon hung up and gripped the steering wheel as he waited impatiently. The wind shook the vehicle as it buffeted it. "What is going on?" Melissa asked.

"I don't know."

"Do you think Cassie is near?"

He was afraid to acknowledge it may very well have been Cassie who had done this. *His* Cassie never could have done this, but there was no way to know what had been done to her. He couldn't admit *his* Cassie might not exist anymore.

"Yes," he admitted.

Annabelle and Liam appeared at the edge of the parking lot and moved rapidly across the snow and asphalt. Devon hit the unlock button and let them into the backseat on a blast of cold air. "What's going on?" Liam asked as soon as he was settled.

Devon quickly filled him in on the condition of the hotel as he pulled out of the parking lot. His headlights splashed over the woods and across the snow. "Where did the people staying in the motel go though?" Annabelle inquired.

Devon had been thinking the same thing as he made his way toward town. "I don't know, but hopefully we'll find some answers soon."

CHAPTER TWENTY

CASSIE HURRIED to the window and knelt upon the bed as she eagerly peered into Julian's room. He was already lying on his bed, his arm tossed over his eyes as he tried to block out the harsh illumination. There were fresh burn marks marring the pale skin of his arms, and his hair was singed at the edges. She didn't know what they had done to him today, but it had been far more than a taser, and Dani.

She gaped at him as she noted more burn marks lining his firm jaw line and cheeks. Her heart constricted; sorrow filled her at the obvious signs of torture he'd endured. These marks could be hours old, which meant he would have had hours of healing behind him already and yet the wounds were still quite visible.

Cassie swallowed heavily; fresh tears stung her eyes as she pressed her hands against the glass. She longed to touch him, to ease the suffering radiating from his body. "I'm ok, Princess."

She started at the sound of his hoarse, strained voice. "How did you know I was here?" she whispered.

"I would know you anywhere."

Cassie hastily wiped away the tears streaming down her face. She knew he would hate them. He would especially hate they were for *him*. Her chest constricted with the strain it took to keep her sob suppressed. "What did they *do* to you?" she breathed, unable to keep the hitch from her voice.

He didn't lower his arm to look at her, didn't turn toward her, but she knew her tone had affected him as a shudder ran through his body. Cassie rested her forehead against the glass; she wished he would talk to her or at least look at her. He seemed beaten, defeated, and she needed him to be strong and positive they would escape this alive.

Finally he turned toward her, but he didn't lower his arm from his eyes. "I'm fine," he mumbled.

"You don't look fine," she retorted. "What did they do?"

He hadn't been in his room when she'd been returned to hers, and though they'd actually taken it somewhat easy on her today, it appeared they hadn't been so kind to Julian. In fact, it seemed they had been twice as brutal to him. He lifted his arm a little to peer up at her. Cassie stared in dismay at the sight of his blood red, swollen, and brutalized eyes. He squinted up at her, his normally lively blue eyes blank. Cassie's hand flew to her mouth as she realized he couldn't see her. He was *blind*.

"Julian," she breathed unable to hold back her tears.

"Don't cry, Princess."

"You can see me?" she gasped in relief.

He shook his head and dropped his arm back over his tortured eyes. "Not for a few more hours. I can smell your tears though. Don't cry over me, I'm not worth it."

Cassie's breath hitched as heartache bloomed through her chest. "Yes, you are," she whispered. "You really are Julian, and don't you *ever* doubt that."

He remained unmoving for a moment, and then his head

turned toward her. He didn't lower his arm, but she knew all of his attention was focused on her. "I'm glad you think so."

Cassie was unable to stop the tears flowing down her cheeks. She knew he hated them, but his torment was more than she could bear. "I *know* so," she whispered. "What did they do to you?"

He stiffened for a moment and then relaxed visibly. "They just wanted to make sure I hadn't picked up Devon's nifty trick for surviving the rays of the sun."

How long had they tortured him after realizing he wasn't capable of moving about in the daytime? "I'm sorry."

"I don't want your pity, Princess," he grated out.

"I'm not pitying you; I'm sorry you had to go through that today. How long did they keep you outside?"

Julian shook his head and shifted a little on the bed. "Didn't go outside, they had one of those UV lamp things."

"How long?"

"I don't know," he mumbled.

Cassie's gaze raked over his lean body. Though he wore scrubs, she knew his legs would be as burned as the rest of him. She didn't know how the UV lights worked, but she bet he'd been subjected to their rays for a while. Sighing heavily, she dropped down on the bed, and rested her head against the glass.

"How was your day dear?"

Cassie couldn't help but smile as she shook her head at him. Though he was in obvious discomfort, he still hadn't completely lost his sense of humor. "Just peachy," she told him. "I think my veins are going to collapse."

"Hmm, I bet. Did they give you another shot?"

Cassie braced herself before looking down at her arms, but there was no discoloration today as her arms remained pale, and needle puckered. "No."

"Hmm," he grunted again. "That's good."

She leaned against the window and pressed her hand to the glass. She missed the imaginary feel of his hand pressed to hers. Resting her cheek against the glass, she stared down at him as a riot of emotions tore through her and made it difficult to breathe. There had to be some way out of here, but she had yet to find a chink in their captor's armor.

"Cassie." She turned back to Julian as she stifled a yawn. His arm was still draped over his eyes, but the burns on his arms looked somewhat better. "We have to get out of here."

"I know. They're going to kill us soon."

"Yes," he agreed. "And one thing I will not survive is the loss of your life."

Cassie tried not to cry harder at his words. She would only bring him misery, but he seemed set in his feelings for her, no matter how much she didn't want them. Or at least she told herself she didn't want them, repeatedly. Julian had made his way into her heart and she loved him in a way she'd never thought possible. He was her friend, her rock, and she needed him. She loved Devon, she really did, but her feelings for Julian were new and strange and confusing.

And she didn't have time to sort through them. Not in here anyway, not until they were free.

Cassie bit on her bottom lip as her gaze shot toward the bigger mirror. She was always concerned they were listening to them, laughing at them for their stupidity at thinking they could escape. But she had to think of a way to get them both out of here, before there was no chance of escape anymore.

She turned back to Julian and winced at the brutal wounds. His pain was her pain; she felt it as acutely as she would have felt her own burns. She had to get him out of here before they destroyed him. She wouldn't survive his loss either. He owned a piece of her heart now, and he always would. She would be broken without him.

Cassie hugged her legs to her chest as her resentment toward this whole awful situation grew. Tears rolled down her face as her thoughts turned to Devon. She longed for him constantly; she missed him more than she would miss the loss of her own arm. Yet she was sitting here, confused, uncertain, and in turmoil because of her growing feelings for Julian. Biting on her bottom lip, she tried to keep her sobs from Julian, but she knew she'd failed miserably when his palm suddenly pressed against the glass.

Cassie knew she shouldn't touch it. She should start to sever the tie between them, but she couldn't bring herself to do so, not now. Not when she was so alone, and frightened, and in need of his strength and love. Not when she knew he required this more than she did. She was being selfish, and she hated herself for it, but she couldn't stop herself from pressing her hand to his.

She buried her face in her knees as her tears flowed freely. She had to get them out of here before she destroyed all of their lives by crossing a line she'd never thought she would. She knew where her heart belonged, who owned her soul, but things were so different in here. Julian was going to be hurt if they ever made it out of here, and Devon wouldn't understand her strange new feelings for a man who had been their worst enemy. No, Devon wouldn't understand it at all, and he may never forgive her for it.

She didn't know if *she* could forgive herself for it.

She curled up against the wall as she kept her hand to the glass. She allowed the drugs to pull her under, grateful for the escape they now offered her.

CHAPTER TWENTY-ONE

CASSIE STARTED awake and blinked rapidly against the drug induced sleep trying to pull her back under. An alarm was blaring somewhere; red lights flashed through the small window in her door. Her forehead furrowed as she tried to puzzle out what was going on, what all the commotion was about.

Shouts filled the air; feet slapped against the tiled floor. Cassie watched as two people raced by. Shoving herself up, she struggled against the drugged stupor clinging to her. She swayed a little and the flashing beams did nothing to help her disorientation and dizziness.

Moving gingerly, she turned toward Julian's room, but it was dark in there now and she couldn't see him. More shouts rang out as a siren began to wail. Fear curdled through her as she staggered toward the door and fell into it. Standing on her tiptoes she watched as another group raced by, heading in the opposite direction of the people she'd seen earlier.

An agonized scream rent the air. All the blood seemed to drop straight into her toes as the wretched scream continued on for a few more seconds before ending abruptly. A fierce shaking wracked her as she stepped away from the door. She didn't know what was going on out there, but it wasn't good.

Stepping back to the door, she rested her hands upon it as more shout's reverberated through the concrete hall. She turned back to Julian's room, but it remained dark and empty. The siren volume increased to the point where it became nearly unbearable. She placed her hands over her ears in an attempt to block out the horrendous noise as she backed up a few more steps.

Panic filled her, confusion and horror swirled through her as another tortured scream rebounded through the halls. She took a deep breath as she tried to stay calm. Maybe this was another form of torment they'd designed for her? Another scream echoed down the hall, and she realized this wasn't some new form of torture, but very real. No one could scream like that, unless they were in real, *agonizing* pain.

She turned and fled over to Julian's window, and climbing onto the bed she began to pound against the glass. She needed him to wake up and help her figure out a way to get out of whatever disaster was occurring right outside their doors. She beat against the glass and screamed his name until her hands throbbed and her throat was raw, but he didn't respond to her.

What if something had already happened to him?

True panic began to fill her as she turned back to the door. More people ran by, their shoes squeaking on the linoleum floor, and their footsteps echoed. She had to get out of here and find Julian. She crept back to the door and strained to see out the window again.

A face suddenly appeared before her. Cassie jumped back as it peered in at her. Its red eyes were filled with rage and insanity as it focused on her. Its lips pulled back from its teeth as it hissed at her. Long fangs cut into its lip and caused blood to pour down its chin, but it seemed oblivious as it stared at her ravenously.

She knew immediately it was one of those things stuck in-between, a monster with no soul and no rational thought. It was the same thing lurking inside of her. Nausea twisted through her, for the first time she was grateful for the thick metal door holding her within this room.

Drool slipped down its chin as it sniffed the air at the edges of the door. She remained frozen in place; she couldn't find the strength to pick up her feet and get away from it. It continued to sniff at her door as it moved across the window. Cassie's breath was trapped in her lungs as the door handle rattled. She waited to see if it could break into the room she hadn't been able to break out of.

The knob rattled more as the thing began to jerk upon it. Excitement radiated from the creature, along with hunger. Cassie braced herself for a fight as she became positive this thing would get into her room. The monstrosity ran on pure bloodlust and destruction, but she wasn't going down without a fight. Cassie's mouth dropped as a bolt of electricity shot down the hall, slammed into the creature, and knocked it back.

Dani appeared before the door, her gold streaked eyes were filled with dread as she met Cassie's gaze. The flashing red alarm lights brought out the blood red streaks in her hair. She fumbled with something before the handle turned and the door was flung open.

"We have to go!" Dani yelled at her when Cassie remained immobile. "Now Cassie! We have to go *now*!"

Cassie stared at her, puzzled and confused by everything that was happening. Then, her survival instincts kicked in. At the moment it didn't matter what Dani had done before, if this was her chance to escape this hellhole, she was going to take it. She stepped into the hall and took in the complicated twists and turns convoluting the place.

"This way!" Dani seized hold of her arm and pulled her to the left.

"Wait! Wait!" Cassie dug her feet in and pulled away from her. "I must find Julian, where is his cell?"

Dani gawked at her. "Cassie we don't have time! We *must* go!"

Cassie defiantly met Dani's horrified gaze. "I'm not leaving here without him!" she yelled over the roaring alarm. Dani shook her head. Cassie grabbed hold of her shirt and pulled her forward as she thrust her face into Dani's. "You helped put me in here! You *will* help me get him out of here!"

Dani's eyes widened as dread flashed through them. "He's a monster."

A sneer curved Cassie's upper lip. "No more than you! Take me to him Dani, or I *will* kill you."

Dani's mouth parted on a small breath as she searched Cassie's face. Cassie stared ferociously back at her, she'd meant every word she'd just said. This girl was the cause of her imprisonment, and she had no problem returning Dani's betrayal with death. Loathing burned in Cassie's stomach, it raced through her veins as her grip on Dani's shirt tightened. She knew she was on the verge of losing all control, and she didn't care.

"Now Dani!" she barked.

Dani licked her lips nervously as she managed a small nod. "Yes, ok, come on." Cassie didn't like putting her faith in the girl again, but she had no other choice. Dani grabbed hold of her hand and squeezed it briefly. "You can trust me Cassie."

A bitter laugh escaped her. "I doubt it."

She released Dani and pushed her back. They stared at each other for a moment before Dani turned and headed in the opposite direction. Cassie followed noiselessly behind, her attention riveted on the hallways. Though the only sound now was the blaring of the siren, she knew there was evil out there, hunting them. Dani broke into a brisk jog and Cassie stayed right on her heels. She was terrified she wouldn't get to Julian in time, and they would all die in here.

Dani skidded around a corner and came to an abrupt halt in front of a door. She nearly dropped the keys on the ground as she searched for the right one. Finally, she slid a key in and turned it. The door swung open to reveal a darkened room. Cassie pushed Dani forward; she didn't trust her enough to leave her in the hall alone.

The red lights pulsated around the room and lit it in disconcerting flashes. Her heightened vision picked out Julian's prone form lying upon his bed. "Give me a hand," she ordered briskly.

"Cassie..."

"Now!" she snarled.

Dani jumped a little but nodded briskly. Cassie hurried toward the bed and grabbed hold of Julian's arm. It was a surprise to actually touch him after all the nights they had spent with a piece of glass between them. His skin was supple and firm beneath her palm, and the fine hairs covering it were somewhat bristly.

He was cooler to the touch, and radiated power like Devon, but unlike when she touched Devon, she didn't feel a rushing sense of rightness. She did, however, feel a sense of relief that nearly choked her. Touching Julian didn't make her feel whole like Devon did, but it did give her a sense of comfort that helped alleviate the suffering and loneliness that had encompassed her in here.

He groaned as Cassie pulled him up and kept a firm hold on his limp form. Readjusting him, she draped his arm around her shoulder and drew on her strength to lift him to his feet. "Help me," she growled to Dani.

Dani hesitated and her terrified eyes flitted to the door. Taking a deep breath, she hurried to Julian's other side and draped his arm around her. "We have to hurry!" Dani said urgently. "They're coming!"

Cassie strained to hear anything above the roaring siren, but it drowned out all other sound. She thought of the monster outside of her room and knew what was coming. Dragging Julian forward, she rushed from the room as quickly as his dead weight would allow her to. She let Dani lead them through the twists and turns with an ease that only infuriated Cassie more. The girl was very comfortable in this hideous place.

Julian's hand twitched in hers, but he showed little signs of rousing. The alarm cut off as the blaring noise ended as abruptly as it had begun. Cassie froze; the sudden hush was more unnerving than the loud blaring had been. "How much further?" Cassie whispered, hating how loud her voice sounded amidst the unnerving hush.

"Not much," Dani murmured. "Come."

Cassie winced as Julian's feet squeaked across the floor; the sound seemed as loud as a gunshot in the unending silence. Another blood curdling scream rent the air. The hair on Cassie's neck stood on end as she glanced behind her. The scream broke off, and then a series of shorter ones began to reverberate through the hall.

Julian twitched again as his head lolled to the side. Cassie glanced apprehensively at him. How much drugs had they pumped into him, and just how much damage had the UV rays done to him? She could only see a few darker burns still marring the skin along his hairline, and his eyes were no longer swollen, but she was certain there were still more marks on him. Cassie's attention was ripped away from him as Dani started down another hallway, briefly pulling Julian behind her. Cassie found her feet again as fright spurred her forward faster.

Julian's hand constricted briefly on hers again. "Wha's goin' on?" he muttered in a slurred voice.

"We're getting out of here," Cassie answered.

His head lolled toward her. "Cassie?" he blurted.

"Shh, we have to be quiet Julian."

He continued to stare blearily at her, and then he shook his head. "No, this isn't real. I must be dreaming, or they've figured out some new experiment."

Sorrow for him filled her. She jerked Dani to a halt as she stopped abruptly. Grasping hold of his chin, she turned his head forcefully toward her. "This is *very* real Julian," she whispered fervently and squeezed his chin to reinforce her words. "I *am* real, and I need your help. You have to start walking otherwise we're not going to get out of this alive!"

His dazed gaze finally focused on her completely. "This is real?"

"Yes, and we have to get out."

He blinked again and his shoulders straightened. He seemed to realize someone else was holding him as he turned away from her. His body became rigid, his grip constricted on her hand as a feral hiss escaped him. Dani's mouth dropped as her eyes flew toward Cassie. Cassie briefly contemplated letting Julian do whatever he wanted to Dani. But no matter how much she disliked the girl, she couldn't allow that to happen. They needed Dani to get out of here, and her conscience wouldn't let Julian kill Dani in cold blood.

"No, Julian," Cassie said as she tugged on his hand. "We need her to get out of here."

Dani's nostrils flared as she grasped the unstated threat

behind Cassie's statement. Once they were free, there were no promises. "Let's go," Dani said.

Julian used his own feet, but he still leaned on her shoulder as they continued forward. He had pulled away from Dani, but continued to watch her with a curved upper lip. They arrived at a set of elevators, but Dani turned away from them and headed to the right. "We must use the stairs," Dani explained in a hushed voice. "I don't trust the elevator to stay working."

They followed her down the hall until they arrived at a set of swinging doors. Dani fumbled with the keys again and unlocked the doors with a shaky hand before shoving through them. Flights of stairs steeply wound their way up. Cassie's shoulders slumped as she stared at the twisting mess before them. She was exhausted, still slightly drugged, and every muscle in her body throbbed from dragging Julian, but she could do this. She *would* do this.

Staggering a little, she helped Julian forward as Dani quickly relocked the doors. Her hand grasped hold of the banister as Julian rested his other hand against the wall. Working together she was able to lead him swiftly up the first two flights before the strain began to truly weigh on her. She labored up the next flight before tripping over a step.

With a muted cry, she fell forward and smashed her knees on the landing. Pain lanced through her, but she shoved it aside as she fought not to let it get the best of her. Julian grasped hold of her arm and helped her back up. "You can do this, Princess," he murmured in her ear.

"Don't call me princess," she retorted.

His familiar cocky grin flitted over his handsome features as his eyes sparked with amusement. "Come on," Dani urged. "There's only one more flight."

Cassie shoved herself back to her feet. Julian kept hold of

her arm as they struggled up the last flight of stairs. Dani hesitated at the top to peer out the window in the large metal door blocking their way.

Taking a deep breath, Dani set her shoulders as she fumbled to get the keys out of her pocket. Cassie watched impatiently as Dani shakily inserted it into the lock and turned the key. They waited breathlessly as she pulled the door open and peeked out. "I think it's safe," she whispered.

Dani opened the door further and slid through it. Cassie stepped through the doors and her breath exploded from her as she took in the locker lined hallway. "What is this?" Julian demanded.

"Cedarville School," Dani answered.

"Where is *Cedarville*?" Cassie demanded.

"Upstate New York."

Cassie glanced rapidly up and down the hall. "You put that monstrosity down there beneath a school?" she grated.

"*I* didn't put it anywhere!" Dani retorted. "And I think we had better get free of here before we have this conversation, don't you?"

Cassie glared back at her, her hands fisted as she fought the urge to punch Dani in her traitorous face. Julian grasped hold of her arm and shook his head at her. "Not here."

Her hands relaxed as she nodded briefly. Dani was watching them in wide eyed fascination. "*What* are you staring at?" Julian grumbled as he stepped protectively in front of Cassie.

Cassie touched his arm as she sought to soothe some of the rage vibrating through him. Julian relaxed as some of the tension eased from him. Dani's eyes shot back and forth between them as horror crept into her gaze. Cassie knew what Dani saw, knew she thought Cassie was betraying Devon, but she couldn't bring herself to care what Dani thought of her. Cassie tilted her chin and glared back at Dani.

Dani's mouth closed as she shook her head. "Come on."

Cassie didn't know if Dani meant the monsters that had held them captive, or the creatures like the one that had tried to get into her room. Either way she didn't care, she just wanted to be free. She followed behind as Dani crept cautiously past the lockers and empty classrooms. Julian was able to move on his own now, but he stayed close enough to Cassie his arm brushed against hers as they moved. They turned a corner and hurried past a gym before making their way into a small cafeteria.

They were halfway through the tables when the hair on the back of Cassie's neck stood on end and a shiver slid down her spine. Her gaze scanned rapidly over the darkened tables and benches as she stopped moving. "Cassie!" Julian barked.

"There's something here," she whispered back.

His eyes flashed briefly red as he moved closer to her. "Where?"

She shook her head and turned helplessly back to him. She couldn't see any threat in the room, but she knew it was there, stalking them. She could feel it amongst the shadows waiting to pounce upon them. Dani was impatiently waiting for them a few feet away. Cassie shook her head as she tried to rid herself of the feeling.

And then, she knew.

Ever so slowly, she tilted her head back. Her heart hammered in trepidation as her mouth instantly went dry. A gasp escaped her when she spotted the thing amongst the beams. Its red eyes gleamed down at her as it watched them with hungry fascination. Julian seized hold of her arm and shoved her out of the way as the thing launched itself from the beams with an eager mewl.

Cassie's hip slammed into the corner of a table. Julian seized hold of the creature's throat as it landed upon him. Flipping the monster over his head, he effortlessly threw it away from him. It flew a good ten feet through the air before crashing into one of the tables. It released a low grunt as it bounced off of the table and slid into the shadows again. Julian turned with the creature as it scurried through the benches and tables with an inhuman agility that stole Cassie's breath.

Dani edged closer to them and huddled by Cassie's side as they all followed the creature's furtive movement through the dark. A bench was knocked aside, and then it seemed to disappear once more. Julian took a step closer to her, blocking her with his large frame. "Stay close!" he commanded.

A table to their left skidded backward causing Dani to brush against her side. Cassie fought the urge to push her away, but Dani was the only reason they'd even made it this far. No matter how cruel Dani had been to them, Cassie couldn't bring herself to be so vindictive to the frightened girl.

A shadow reared up out of the night as it launched itself at them. A scream caught in Cassie's throat as it snagged hold of Dani's arm and an eager hiss escaped it. Dani screamed loudly, and threw her hands up in a useless attempt to dislodge the creature. Cassie tried to pull Dani away as the thing clawed at her arm and tore her sweatshirt to shreds. Strange noises escaped from it, its misshapen teeth snapped as it tried to latch onto Dani's neck.

Julian lurched toward them in a rushing blur, but Cassie was quicker. Reacting on instinct alone, she drove her fist into the creature's cheek and knocked its head to the side. With it temporarily knocked off balance, Cassie was able to rip Dani out of the away and shove her aside.

Cassie relished in the anger boiling forward and the

powerful surge that came with it. Leaping over the table, she caught hold of the thing's leg before it scurried into the darkness again. It howled as it rounded on her. For a moment it seemed to hesitate as its eyes caught sight of her. Cassie hesitated as confusion swirled through her. Devon had said these things had no reasonable thought, no survival instinct but this thing seemed rational for a brief second.

Then it was coming at her, moving with inhuman speed as it lashed out with inhuman looking claws. Cassie dodged the blow, and jerked the monstrosity back by the ankle. It howled as it clawed at the floor for purchase to get away from her.

"Cassie!" Julian shouted.

She felt him at her shoulder milliseconds before she drove her fist into the thing's chest. Bone crunched beneath her hand and was driven in as it gave out completely. The creature screamed, and its hands shoved at her as it tried to dislodge her.

Julian leapt over the top of the monstrosity in one single leap. Landing behind it, he seized hold of its head and ripped it to the side in a violent, jerking motion. The loud sound of bone shattering echoed throughout the room. The thing squealed and staggered back as its head twisted disgustingly to the side on its broken neck.

Julian's eyes were bright red as they met hers. "Turn away!" he snarled at her. Cassie blinked in surprise, but she was unable to move. "Cassie, *turn* around!"

She came out of her haze as she turned away. She stumbled as she fought the desperate urge to flee this place and never look back. Lingering remnants of adrenaline and revulsion coursed through her. For one horrifying moment, she had truly enjoyed fighting the creature and destroying it. For the first time since she'd been placed in this awful place, she was finally feeling the *real* Cassie bubbling beneath the surface again, and she was appalled and terrified by it.

Dani grasped hold of her arms and pulled her forward as the thing began to squeal again. Cassie hugged herself against the inhuman squeals of pain and terror. A sickening crunch and a squishing noise finally silenced the pathetic thing.

"Are you ok?" Cassie glanced up as Julian appeared at her side; his reddened eyes were narrowed as he surveyed the cuts marring Cassie and Dani's arms. Cassie gazed down at the scratches on her arms, but she barely noticed the blood seeping from them. Julian cast Dani a scathing look as he pulled Cassie gently away from her. Turning her arms, he tenderly fingered the jagged gashes.

"I'm fine," she assured him.

His eyes were still a violent shade of red, but there was a softening in his features. "You're in control?"

She frowned at him. "Of course I am."

His hands cupped her face and lifted it toward him. "Your eyes are red."

Cassie's mouth parted on a breath. Instinctively, she jerked away from him as she backed up a couple of steps. She needed to flee; she needed to get far away before she injured one of them. "What?"

"Cassie..."

Dani came at her, but Cassie kept back peddling until she came up against a chair. Her knees gave out; she sat heavily on the chair as her breath rushed out of her in a loud whoosh. "Get away!" she cried.

Julian gripped her arms so tight she winced in response. "Cassie, stop!"

She fisted her hands and closed her eyes against the impending wave of hatred that would soon swamp her body. It would consume her again and leave her twisting in agony, useless, and on the verge of becoming a monster. "You can fight against this," Julian told her as he placed her palms against the solid muscles of his chest.

She was braced for the pain to rise up, but it didn't come, and the longer Cassie sat there the more she realized it wasn't coming. Though she'd been frightened and angry, she didn't feel the loss of control that had enveloped her when she'd killed Isla. This time she'd been motivated by survival instinct, it had been pure reaction and adrenaline filling her.

But she'd been fueled by those things before, and her eyes had never turned red. She'd never exhibited the same kind of physical strength she had when she'd demolished the creature's chest, at least not before Isla.

A cold chill swept down Cassie's spine as ice filled her veins. She couldn't breathe, and she truly feared she might pass out. Then, the air came back into her chest and the feeling returned to her muscles. Her hands clenched upon Julian's as she met Dani's troubled gaze.

"What did they do to us in there?" Cassie breathed.

"Cassie..." Dani started.

"What did they do to *me* in there?" she demanded as she rose off of the chair.

"I don't know," Dani answered. "But we must go Cassie. There are more of them, *many* more. We need to go."

Cassie looked back at Julian as she fought the tears filling her eyes. "Come on Cassie," he said forcefully.

She blinked back the tears and nodded. She was unable to stand this strange new world without his comfort. She kept both of her hands wrapped around his right one as he weaved gracefully through the tables. Dani reached one of the emergency doors and flung it open on the winter night. Cassie's scrubs were little protection against the howling wind, her bare feet froze immediately, but it was the most fantastic thing she'd ever felt in her life.

Free! They were *free*! Stumbling outside, Cassie nearly fell to her knees. She almost sobbed with joy as she inhaled heaping gulps of blessedly fresh air. Julian turned toward her, a radiant smile on his magnificent face. The moon played over his handsome features and lit the beautiful blue of his eyes.

She couldn't help but return his jubilant smile as her heart leapt in her chest. Julian's brilliant smile made him appear so innocent and joyful. He pulled her forward and drew her flush against his chest. Before Cassie could react, his head bent to hers and his lips seized hold of hers. Cassie's gasp of surprise allowed his tongue access to her mouth.

Unable to move beneath the tender press of his lips and tongue, a fresh rush of emotions tore through her. She wanted to pull away from the wrongness of his kiss, but there was something that didn't feel so wrong about it. Desire and belonging didn't pool through her like it did with Devon, but a strange swell of love bloomed within her as tears slipped down her cheeks. Though this was not right, in a strange way it *was*, which only served to confuse and unnerve her more.

Julian pulled away, and his hand caressed her cheek. Cassie stared at him wordlessly as awe and anguish filled her. She was an awful person, horrendous. Devon *never* would have kissed another person. He *never* would have considered it. Yet she'd just kissed Julian, or he'd kissed her, but she'd returned it with more feeling than she'd thought possible.

He was staring at her with such sadness and understanding, it broke her heart.

Anger and self-loathing washed through her as she met Dani's appalled gaze. She was so awful she was even being judged by Dani now, one of the worst forms of human life Cassie had ever encountered. Her fingers lingered over her lips as she glanced helplessly back at Julian. She loved him, she truly did, but it wasn't the same as Devon, it could never be the same.

Julian's fingers stroked over her cheek once more. His forehead rested against hers. "Julian," she breathed.

His eyes closed as his hand briefly tensed on her face. "I know Cassie, I know. I just *needed* it."

She was glad he knew, because she sure didn't. As wispy as a butterfly's caress, his lips brushed over hers once more before he reluctantly pulled away. She remained staring up at him, unaware of the cold wind beating against them. He smiled as he pinched her cheek lightly and used his humor as a defense again.

"Come on, Princess let's get as far away from this shithole as we can."

Before she could respond, or stop to think what that kiss had meant to her, what Julian knew, or what her feelings about this situation were, Julian was tugging her forward. They sprinted across an open baseball field before finally reaching the sanctuary of the woods. She didn't know what was awaiting them out here, nor did she care. She was just happy to be free, to be breathing fresh air, no matter how cold or uncertain the world surrounding them was.

She clung to Julian's hand as they plunged into the forest. They had to get free of this town, and she had to find Devon, soon. She had to know he was safe, and she had to ease the torment she was certain he was going through just as she required him to ease the tumult of emotions and confusion within her.

She studied the man before her as he led her easily through

the trees, his hand strong and sure in hers. Though she tried to deny it, she knew her feelings for him were not entirely platonic. She may not feel the same way about him she felt about Devon, but there was definitely something there. She could only hope she wouldn't be more confused about her feelings for Julian when she finally got the chance to see Devon again.

The End

∾

Book 4, *Inferno*, is now available!
***Inferno* on Amazon: ericastevensauthor.com/Infwb**

Stay in touch on updates and new releases from the author by joining the mailing list!
Mailing list for Erica Stevens & Brenda K. Davies Updates:
ericastevensauthor.com/ESBKDNews

FIND THE AUTHOR

Erica Stevens/Brenda K. Davies Mailing List:
ericastevensauthor.com/ESBKDNews

Facebook page: ericastevensauthor.com/ESfb

Erica Stevens/Brenda K. Davies Book Club:
ericastevensauthor.com/ESBKDBookClub

Instagram: ericastevensauthor.com/ESinsta
Twitter: ericastevensauthor.com/EStw
Website: ericastevensauthor.com
Blog: ericastevensauthor.com/ESblog
BookBub: ericastevensauthor.com/ESbkbb

ABOUT THE AUTHOR

Erica Stevens is the author of the Captive Series, Coven Series, Kindred Series, Fire & Ice Series, Ravening Series, and the Survivor Chronicles. She enjoys writing young adult, new adult, romance, horror, and science fiction. She also writes adult paranormal romance and historical romance under the pen name, Brenda K. Davies. When not out with friends and family, she is at home with her husband, son, dog, cat, and horse.

ALSO FROM THE AUTHOR

Books written under the pen name

Erica Stevens

The Coven Series

Nightmares (Book 1)

The Maze (Book 2)

Dream Walker (Book 3)

The Captive Series

Captured (Book 1)

Renegade (Book 2)

Refugee (Book 3)

Salvation (Book 4)

Redemption (Book 5)

Broken (The Captive Series Prequel)

Vengeance (Book 6)

Unbound (Book 7)

The Kindred Series

Kindred (Book 1)

Ashes (Book 2)

Kindled (Book 3)

Inferno (Book 4)

Phoenix Rising (Book 5)

The Fire & Ice Series

Frost Burn (Book 1)

Arctic Fire (Book 2)

Scorched Ice (Book 3)

The Ravening Series

The Ravening (Book 1)

Taken Over (Book 2)

Reclamation (Book 3)

The Survivor Chronicles

The Upheaval (Book 1)

The Divide (Book 2)

The Forsaken (Book 3)

The Risen (Book 4)

Books written under the pen name
Brenda K. Davies

The Vampire Awakenings Series

Awakened (Book 1)

Destined (Book 2)

Untamed (Book 3)

Enraptured (Book 4)

Undone (Book 5)

Fractured (Book 6)

Ravaged (Book 7)

Consumed (Book 8)

Unforeseen (Book 9)

Forsaken (Book 10)

Relentless (Book 11)

Coming Fall 2020

The Alliance Series

Eternally Bound (Book 1)

Bound by Vengeance (Book 2)

Bound by Darkness (Book 3)

Bound by Passion (Book 4)

Bound by Torment (Book 5)

Coming Spring 2020

The Road to Hell Series

Good Intentions (Book 1)

Carved (Book 2)

The Road (Book 3)

Into Hell (Book 4)

Hell on Earth Series

Hell on Earth (Book 1)

Into the Abyss (Book 2)

Kiss of Death (Book 3)

The Edge of the Darkness

Coming Summer 2020

Historical Romance

A Stolen Heart

Printed in Great Britain
by Amazon

82880216R00149